"I think it's time for you to kiss me again."

He looked at her, a mixture of emotions flashing across his features. "Forget it, Abby. You don't want to go kissing a guy like me. There's no future in it."

Future! "Guys like you are the only kind worth kissing," she said lightly, hoping he didn't detect her disappointment at his words. She refused to believe he didn't feel any attraction toward her. After all, he did kiss her earlier that evening. Thinking of that made her breath come a little faster. No one had ever kissed her that way.

"Abby, you deserve a man who will treat you right. A man who can provide you with a future, someone you have things in common with."

"Maybe you're right. Maybe I do deserve some mythical paragon of excellence. But I don't want that, Daniel." She touched his cheek and smiled. "I want you. Now why don't you just shut up and kiss me?"

And finally, that's exactly what he did.

RAYE MORGAN

has spent almost two decades, while writing
over fifty novels, searching for the answer to that
elusive question: just what is that special magic that
happens when a man and a woman fall in love?
Every time she thinks she has the answer, a new
wrinkle pops up, necessitating another book!
The LOGAN'S LEGACY series gave her another
chance to explore the subject—this time with an
emphasis on the humor of the situation. What
happens when Detective Daniel O'Callahan finds
himself falling for Abby Edwards, who seems
to be promoting a product that turns people into
love-zombies? Raye had a lot of fun finding out!
Meanwhile, after living in Holland, Guam, Japan
and Washington, D.C., she currently makes her
home in Southern California with her husband
and two of her four boys.

LOGAN'S LEGACY
UNDERCOVER PASSION
RAYE MORGAN

Silhouette Books

Published by Silhouette Books
America's Publisher of Contemporary Romance

Special thanks and acknowledgment are given
to Raye Morgan for her contribution
to the LOGAN'S LEGACY series.

 SILHOUETTE BOOKS

ISBN 0-373-61398-9

UNDERCOVER PASSION

Be a part of

$\mathcal{L}$ogan's $\mathcal{L}$egacy

*Because birthright has its privileges
and family ties run deep.*

**An undercover detective wants to find the
reason for strange behavior in the hospital.
Can he keep his mission secret as he falls
for a woman closely involved in his work?**

Daniel O'Callahan: While unraveling the mystery
behind Dr. Richie, this detective investigated his
attraction to the doctor's PR representative,
Abby Edwards. Her sparkling smile and sweet
demeanor enchanted him and made his assignment
even harder!

Abby Edwards: She'd never given much thought
to mind-numbing romance because her career
seemed more rewarding. But the thunderbolt
hit her when she met Daniel and he made her
dream of those once unreachable goals such
as family and love.

A Man Exposed: Once his past was revealed,
Dr. Richie ran off to parts unknown. Could his
long-lost wife's forgiveness redeem this broken man?

THE SOLUTION YOU'VE BEEN WAITING FOR...

THE REMEDY YOU DESERVE...

NoWAIT

THE AMAZING NEW DIET OIL. USE IT AND WATCH THE POUNDS MELT AWAY!

NoWait: A little rub on the skin, and in no time you're thin!

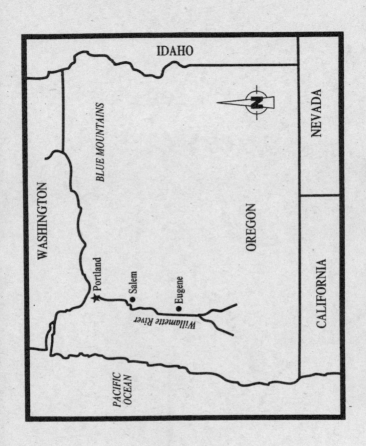

One

Daniel O'Callahan had eyes as cold and clear as the emeralds they resembled. He also had the mind typical of a hard-headed detective and a natural instinct for trouble.

"There's something fishy going on here," he muttered to himself, giving his grandmother a hello kiss on the cheek as she lay back in her hospital bed. He turned to stare coolly at the cute little redheaded nurse giving him the eye from the doorway.

"Oh, no, dear," his grandmother responded

cheerfully. "That's just the remnants of my tuna sandwich. It made a lovely lunch."

"Right," he said, not bothering to explain what he'd meant.

Instead, he took a few steps into the doorway and glanced up and down the corridor. Three pairs of eyes turned to stare at him from the nurses' station. Giggling could be heard. Then, from the other direction, a low wolf whistle. He turned quickly but only caught the tail end of a candy striper's skirt as she disappeared into another room. The giggling got louder.

He pulled back into the room, frowning. A tall man in top physical condition, with a steely gaze and a chiseled chin, Daniel was used to getting a reaction. Shifty characters tended to draw back into the shadows as he passed, hoping he wouldn't notice them. Women pulled children a bit closer. Men stepped aside to give him room. When he spoke, others listened as though for instructions on what to do next. All that was routine—at least to Daniel.

But this was different. This was something out of step, unbalanced, completely whacked. He'd never caused women to peer at him and giggle before in his life. It wasn't normal, and that, along with the weird behavior he'd noticed around the hospital lately since his elderly relative had checked in, needed investigating.

He was a cop, wasn't he? It was high time he did his job—even if he was on temporary administrative leave from the department while he waited to be cleared of charges of theft during an arrest.

Daniel gazed down at his pretty little gray-haired grandmother, thinking the situation over.

"Listen, Gram, have you told anyone here what I do for a living?"

"That you're a regular old gumshoe? No, I don't think so." Phoebe O'Callahan's eyes brightened and she dropped into a loud whisper. "What's up? Are you on a case? Can I help?"

Daniel gazed at the grandmother who had often been more mother to him than anything else and felt a bit of his tension melt away. You couldn't look at Phoebe and not want to smile.

"Not a case exactly. But I've got something I want to look into and it might help if people didn't know I was a police detective."

"Oh, goodie." She pulled herself up against the pillows, her blue eyes sparkling. "What can I do?"

Daniel sighed and half laughed. He took his grandmother's blue-veined hand in his larger paw and looked at her lovingly. She'd had a very scary fall the day before and he'd brought her in for observation. The doctors had found some problems and since she'd had numerous problems that required hospitalization lately, including a major threat to her hip, she was staying indefinitely while they ran tests and gave her time to recuperate.

"Your job—should you choose to accept it— is to heal those bruises and get yourself well again. That's what you should be concentrating on."

"Oh, Danny, come on," she fretted. "I want to help. Give me a hint. What's this all about?"

Daniel shook his head. He loved his grandmother, but he was beginning to sense the parameters of a conundrum looming, and when he was working he didn't usually brook much frivolity. The trouble was, a certain type of frivolity was exactly what seemed to be going on here.

To put it bluntly, the place seemed to have been infected by a love virus—and a pretty nasty one at that. Everywhere you looked, people were billing and cooing. It was pretty disturbing— enough to put you off romance for life.

Just that morning, when he'd dropped by to see how his grandmother had made it through the night, a very angular and heavily made-up occupational therapist had asked him with much batting of eyes if he'd like to share a doughnut she'd saved for him. The cute redheaded nurse had told him he was too handsome to be running around loose, and a tiny little volunteer had offered to give him a neck rub. Women didn't do that to him. He wasn't the type. It was just plain weird.

He'd been asking around, trying to find what had changed to bring on this wave of everyone acting like dopey survivors from a sixties love-in. No one admitted to knowing what he was talking about. But the one thing he did know was that a new center had been opened on the hospital campus. He'd been at the ribbon-cutting ceremony, just by accident. Called the Healthy Living Clinic, it seemed to be a fitness center and it was definitely the subject of most of the buzz he heard around the halls. Something told him there was a connection. It might be time to give the clinic a visit.

"Let's just say I've got a professionally open mind," he said to Phoebe. "But suspicion is lurking in the corners of it."

* * *

Abby Edwards closed her eyes and took a very deep breath. She had to get hold of herself. This was no time to panic. Just because she'd locked herself in the supply closet on the first full day in her new office at the Healthy Living Clinic didn't mean she was going to prove to the world what a dunderheaded incompetent she was.

"It could have happened to anyone," she murmured gloomily, trying to convince herself. "Anyone at all."

Anyone with a disabled attention span and a brand-new inferiority complex that was growing like an overeating teenager.

"Oh!" she cried, rejecting the defeatism with all her might. "Never mind that. What I need is a plan."

A plan. A plan.

She looked around at the shelves of paper, the boxes of paper clips, the stack of shiny brochures touting the benefits of the Healthy Living Clinic and Dr. Richie's approach to total health and well-being. You'd think someone would have thought to stock a few tools along with the office supplies. If she could just find a screwdriver, she could go to work on the door hinges and make her escape.

This was so infuriating! She'd arrived this morning so full of excitement, determined to show Dr. Richie that he'd made a good move when he'd decided to take her up on her proposal to revamp his entire public relations operation. It had taken all the nerve she had to put together that presentation and approach the doctor on her own, much less demand larger office space to work in. She wasn't used to fighting for that sort of thing. Success had always come easily to her in the past.

That was until she'd opened her own public relations firm. Somehow, as though she'd come under some sort of evil spell, she hadn't managed to do one thing right and her business had failed.

Failed! The word made her gasp, even just thinking it. Failure just wasn't possible. If her parents had any inkling…

No, she told herself fiercely. You cannot cry just because you've messed up again.

Still, she had to wonder. If there was no one there to see you cry, did it really matter?

Yes, it did, she decided. Tears were a sign of weakness. The first step toward that very failure she was so scared of. And she could not afford to fail at this job.

She shook away that nightmare thought. Her luck was supposed to have changed. Developing this new campaign for Dr. Richie was going to fix everything. If she ever got out of the supply closet.

"Hello. Anybody here?"

She froze, listening. Someone had come into the office. Decision time. Was she ready to reveal her pathetic mistake?

"Gone to lunch, I guess," a male voice muttered.

She smiled her relief. She didn't recognize the voice. There would be no problem if a stranger rescued her. Saved at last!

"Hello," she called out. "I'm in here."

After a pause, the voice spoke again. "In where?"

"In the supply closet. I'm locked in, actually. There's no handle on this side. If you could just open the doors..."

A sharp click was followed by one of the doors opening slowly. Looking up, she found herself face to face with a very large, steel-jawed man with a suspicious look in his green eyes.

"What are you doing in there?" he asked abruptly.

Abby stiffened and her eyes narrowed. She'd been ready to be grateful. Honest she had. She'd been ready to smile and thank her rescuer with all her heart.

But there was something about the way he looked at her and the suspicious tone in his voice that set her off. She'd been through a lot in the last fifteen minutes, even if it was mostly in her own head. A little sympathetic treatment would have been just the thing. Instead, she got skepticism. Frustrated, and feeling awfully defensive, she reacted a little hastily to his obvious distrust.

"Who, me?" she said, knowing she sounded flippant but not caring very much. "Checking for termites, of course. I always lock myself in closets so I can catch the little buggers unaware."

"Really." He wasn't moving aside and he filled the opening. His icy green eyes had a penetrating intensity. She felt, for a second or two, as if she was being X-rayed. "Find any?"

Her chin rose. "Not yet." She knew she should smile right now. It was time to make friends, not war.

You catch more flies with honey than with vinegar, Abby. The phrase in her mother's voice echoed in her head, but there was something so annoying about the way this man had jumped to the conclusion that she was up to no good, she just couldn't make use of it.

"I *have* found evidence of other pests, however," she said pointedly, flashing him a look. "I'm hoping I won't have to call an exterminator."

To his credit, one corner of his wide mouth quirked with the tiniest sign of amusement at her jibe.

"So you actually belong here?" he asked, still looking skeptical.

"You thought I was looting the place and got caught in the closet?" She resisted rolling her eyes, though she felt like doing it. "Sorry to disappoint you. I work here."

"Do you?" He paused just long enough to increase her fury. "I was at the ribbon-cutting ceremony last month. Dr. Richie was there. Along with all the counselors and administrators of the clinic and even a few from the hospital." He raised one dark, sleek eyebrow. "I didn't see you there."

She pursed her lips, wondering what he'd do

if she just let go and launched herself at his throat. "It would have been pretty strange if you'd seen me there. I didn't attend. I was out of town."

"Ah."

He didn't believe her? What was he, a security guard she hadn't run across in her few weeks working here? If so, maybe they needed a seminar on employee-to-employee relations.

"So now you've decided I'm a burglar?"

"I don't know what you are. I'm just wondering why you're in this closet."

She'd had enough of this. If he wasn't going to move, she was going to have to scrunch past him. Setting her jaw, she did just that and looked up defiantly.

"I'm not in it anymore. Happy?"

He turned, following her progress across the office, and she had second thoughts. Didn't security guards usually wear uniforms, or at least a badge of some sort? He didn't have either. And if he worked here, he should know about her. Shouldn't he?

Reaching out, she grabbed the brass nameplate from her desk and held it up for him to see.

"This is me. Abby Edwards. Public Relations.

And this is my office." She set the plate back down and fixed him with a stare, folding her arms across her chest. "Can I help you with something?"

He shrugged, jamming his hands down into the pockets of his jacket and looking her over in a way she found particularly insolent.

"What exactly *were* you doing in there?" he asked, giving the closet a quick scan before looking back at her. "Besides the termites, I mean."

She met his gaze levelly, but she had a moment of unease. Could he possibly be someone in the chain of command here at the clinic—someone she should be treating like a boss? But no. It seemed unlikely. He just didn't have the right look. She could relax and give as good as she got.

"Hmm. Just what was I doing in that supply closet?" She pretended to think it over for half a second. "I'd say it was pretty obvious to anyone who was paying attention. Dealing with supplies would have been my first choice. Still, others may differ."

"These supplies?" He indicated the piles stacked around the edge of the office. "That's a lot of stuff to move." He looked at her assessingly. "Tell you what. I'll help you."

She frowned. What the heck was this guy's game, anyway? He'd come out of nowhere and now he wanted to help. If he was so suspicious of her, maybe she ought to return the favor.

"Wait a minute. Who are you exactly?"

He hesitated, then held out his hand. "Name's Daniel O'Callahan," he said shortly. "Nice to meet you, Abby Edwards."

She glanced at his hand. It looked strong and tanned, the fingers long and tapered, the nails neat and even. For a split second, she considered refusing to shake hands with him. But she knew immediately that would be a mistake. Hey, she was supposed to be spreading good feeling, not making enemies. Gritting her teeth, she put her slender hand in his and felt a jolt as his warmth enveloped her.

She pulled her hand back a little too quickly and immediately regretted it when she saw the glint of humor in his eyes. Now he was laughing at her. This was possibly the most infuriating man she'd ever dealt with in her life.

"You still haven't explained what *you* are doing here," she said sharply.

"Haven't I?" He grinned at her, going into a casual slouch that showed how very relaxed he was. By now his body language was telling her that he was completely at home and obviously feeling in control of things.

"No, you haven't. Why don't you tell me what you want and I'll try to direct you to the office where they can help you." There you go. Maybe she could get rid of him.

"What do most people who come to this clinic want?" he countered.

"To improve their lives," she said promptly. "To attain a natural state of well-being through nutritional counseling, a fitness regimen and self-awareness instruction."

He shrugged. "Count me in."

She studied him for a long moment, glanced at the tight, narrow set of his hips, the thigh muscles that bulged beneath the fabric of his slacks, then back at the cocky set of his shoulders and head.

Nope. She just wasn't buying it.

Of course, it was conceivable that the look of fitness and assurance was just a facade. Perhaps beneath that cocky exterior lay a hidden supply of raging neuroses. It was possible that this was all a front to hide his insecurities.

Possible, but not very likely. Not with that look in his eyes.

"What aspect of our services would you be interested in?" she asked him incredulously.

"The whole rigmarole I guess. Tell me about it." Snagging an office chair, he swung down into the seat, stretching his long legs out in front of him. "Do you have a brochure of your product line?"

"Yes. But it's not current. We're having new ones printed up that are more informative." One of her main projects since she'd been hired earlier in the summer had been to revamp the marketing plan. "Tell you what. If you come to the seminar tomorrow night, I'll make sure you get a copy of the new ones."

His nod was saying, "Okay," but the look on his face was saying that wasn't going to satisfy him. "Why not just give me a brief rundown right now?"

She hesitated. "I hate to try to do that." She slumped down into the chair behind the desk, then leaned toward him confidentially. "Okay, I'll be honest with you. Everything is in chaos right now. Once I get moved into this office and have a chance to go over the inventory and the scheduling routines, I'll be able to give you a clearer picture. In the meantime…"

Reaching out, she picked up a flyer and handed it to him. "There you go. Seven-thirty on Tuesday, in the Blue Bayou Room." Spinning in her chair, she took another look at the piles she still had to deal with.

"Now if you'll excuse me, I've got a lot of work ahead of me here."

Daniel gazed at her speculatively. He knew he'd just been dismissed, but he wasn't going anywhere. He hadn't succeeded in getting any closer to the truth about what was going on at this clinic, but at least he'd made a start. Developing a relationship with Abby Edwards, PR person, should give him a lot of access to the inner workings of the place. Besides, he had to admit, he didn't mind the view.

She hadn't seemed all that attractive at first. Despite her luxuriously long brown hair and her deep-brown eyes with the golden flecks, she wasn't classically beautiful. In fact, his initial reaction had been negative. She'd come across as a know-it-all with a chip on her shoulder.

But once she'd settled down and started talking about her work here at the clinic, her natural warmth had taken over and her face had become animated in a way that was quite winning.

Abby Edwards wasn't so bad.

Still, she very much wasn't his type.

What was his type exactly? Hard to tell. A picture of Charlene flashed in his mind but he shoved it away. No, Charlene wasn't his type either. Experience had borne that out. In fact, he probably didn't have a type. He was just a guy wedded to his job. The fact that that job might be in jeopardy right now made that situation all the more bittersweet.

"You know I'm really interested in the work this clinic does," he told her. "And I don't want to wait until tomorrow. Do you have any samples around that I could take a look at?"

"Samples?" She turned back, blinking at him. "Of what?"

"Your products. I understand you have a line of vitamins, for one thing."

"Oh, sure. The vitamins are very popular. In fact, last year they outsold one of the national brands in the hospital pharmacy."

Last year. That wasn't going to help his search. Whatever was going on here, it seemed to be of recent vintage. The vitamins didn't appear to be contenders. He was looking for something new, something that had just been introduced lately.

"I'll have to look into those vitamins," he said smoothly. "In the meantime, have you got anything else?" Anything that might make a whole population of hospital workers turn into love-crazed androids? "Any elixirs? Love potions? Aphrodisiacs? Libido revivers?"

To his surprise, she reddened. "Hey, if you're looking for Viagra," she began indignantly.

He straightened, horrified. "No, no!" Now he felt himself reddening, and that hadn't happened in years. "That's not what I meant."

She bit her lip, then leaned toward him, losing the outrage and looking sympathetic.

"Not that there's anything wrong with that," she said quickly. "If that's your problem, I'm sure that a regimen of exercise will really help. But you might want to consult a sex therapist."

He groaned. "No, wait—"

"It's a common problem. Please don't feel that you have to hide it."

"Hide it!" He choked. This was getting him in deeper and deeper. It wasn't funny. Well, maybe a little bit. But at the same time, it was damned humiliating.

"I don't have a problem," he told her forcefully. "Listen, you took it wrong. I've never had any trouble…." His voice faded out. Looking at her sweet, innocent face, he just couldn't say it. "That way," he said lamely at last. "Really. I'm a normal, healthy male."

She was still looking sympathetic. Damn it all, she thought he was just covering up his embarrassment. There was definitely a good way to prove that she was wrong, but he didn't think she'd go for it. So he stared at her in frustrated silence, wondering how the conversation had taken a turn down this blind alley.

"I can give you a referral," she was saying, digging through the papers on her desk for a note pad.

Reaching out, he grabbed her hand. "I don't need a referral," he said firmly. "I don't need therapy. All I want to know is what sort of products you dispense here besides vitamins."

She was staring at him in bewilderment and he

didn't blame her. He was coming darn close to shouting, and that wasn't going to help anything. He forced a smile, knowing it must look pretty ghastly.

"Hey," he said, remembering something and releasing her hand. "Dr. Richie was saying something about a new product at the ribbon cutting last month. Something called NoGo or Nutrait or—"

"NoWait!" she chimed in, beaming with relief. "Yes, that is a new homeopathic oil he's developed himself. He's such a genius."

"That's the one."

"Oh, it's flying off the shelves. It's used for weight loss, and people are getting the most wonderful results."

Right. He knew a little something about these snake-oil salesmen. If the oil was doing anything, it was through the power of suggestion, no doubt about it. Still, this could be the missing link he'd been looking for. Except for one thing. As he remembered, it wasn't something people took into their system in the usual way.

"It's not ingested, is it?"

"Oh, no." She smiled. "In fact, it's kind of cute. You put a dab behind your ear."

That pretty much shot down his hopes. If you didn't drink it or eat it, how could it change the way you acted to the extent it seemed to be changing the people he was seeing all over the hospital?

"One ear or both?" he asked with a rueful smile.

She blinked. "Tell you the truth, I'm not really sure. I haven't tried it myself." She scrunched her nose at him. "And I hardly think you need to lose any weight."

"You never know," he said quickly, not wanting to go back to speculating on what he *might* be needing help with again. "I'm not getting any younger. And you know how weight tends to accumulate as you age."

"Oh, sure." She was nothing if not understanding. "You can never start working on fitness too early."

He nodded. She was charming when she started talking about the things she felt most passionately about. She sort of lit up with an inner glow that was quite appealing. He wondered, fleetingly, if there was a man in her life. But he dismissed the thought as soon as it formed. Despite her spunk, Abby was soft and sweet and seemingly naive—all the things he wasn't. The women he dated tended to be the women he met in the course of his workday, and as a cop, he mostly mixed with a fairly rough level of society. He wouldn't know what to do with a woman like this.

"So tell me about the exercise programs. What are they like?"

She perked up markedly, her eyes brilliant. "Now those I have tried. They're great, really the most comprehensive I've found anywhere. That was what made me so interested in joining Dr. Richie. I admire him so much. He's been able to do what is so difficult to do—marry serious health advantages with movements that are just really fun and relaxing to do."

Daniel raised an eyebrow. "But can he walk on water?"

She looked startled. "What?"

"Nothing. I was just being rude."

The way her face was shining as she spoke of the good doctor, Daniel felt a twinge of jealousy. Though he would face death rather than admit it.

"How much do you know about this Richie character?"

She drew herself up sternly. "Dr. Richie is a well-respected expert in the fitness field. It's a real honor to get this opportunity to work with him."

She was cute in her righteous indignation, and he had trouble not grinning at her again. Could it be the exercises that were making people act crazy? It didn't seem likely. But he couldn't afford to overlook anything just because it didn't fit the pattern he expected.

"How about a demonstration of the exercises?"

"What— Right now?"

"Can you think of a better time?"

"Well, if you come to the seminar…"

"I'll come to the seminar. But I'd like to get a hint of what I'm letting myself in for."

She frowned. She didn't want to do it. She glanced at her piles of supplies, still languishing on the floor, and he knew she wanted to get things finished here. But she was too polite to say so, and he actually felt a twinge of guilt over putting her in this position. But it was just a twinge. He could easily ignore it.

"Okay," she said, just a hint of her reluctance

showing. Then she visibly put all that behind her and got into the swing of things. "Tell you what. I'll do it if you help."

Her smile was impudent. And that made him suspicious.

"What? How can I help?"

"I know some really fun things for two people to do together," she said happily.

He forced back a laugh. He knew a few fun things for two people to do together, too, but he had a feeling they weren't what she had in mind.

"Don't worry," she told him. "I'll show you what to do."

Reaching under her desk, she pulled out a large exercise mat and plopped it down in the middle of the room. "Okay, we are now going to demonstrate the Giaza."

He was skeptical. He'd much rather watch than join in. "What is the Giaza?"

"It's a set of exercises."

"Sounds more like a set of steak knives."

Grabbing his hand, she pulled him to his feet. "Come on, mister. You asked for it, you got it. Come sit down cross-legged."

"Like this?" He did as she'd ordered.

"You're nice and limber, aren't you? And athletic, I'll bet."

He muttered something. For no known reason, he was suddenly feeling a little self-conscious.

"Okay," he said, settling down, hands on his knees. He was glad he'd worn fairly loose slacks. "What's next?"

"This is the two-person routine. I'm going to sit down, too. We'll be back to back."

That seemed odd. "No kidding."

"No kidding." She stood before him and held her hands together in front of her stomach, looking like an Asian princess. "This is a way to center yourself and prepare for a more strenuous workout. It's mind over matter. See if you can tune into the wavelength where I'm floating."

Oh, brother. Psychobabble. Still, he'd better keep his caustic comments to himself if he didn't want to get kicked out of her office.

"Okay," he said gruffly. "What happens if I bump into you?"

She started to ask him what he meant, then stopped when she no doubt realized he was referring to the floating thing. She gave him a wry look instead and he had to give her points for getting it.

"Our spiritual selves don't bump," she said lightly as she began to lower herself behind him. "They melt right into each other."

"Hmm." For some reason that appealed to him.

She settled in against him. "See? Back to back."

"'And belly to belly,'" he muttered to himself.

"What?"

"Nothing. This just reminds me of an old folk song. About zombies."

He could feel her stiffen.

"Listen, I don't know what you've heard, but this clinic does not turn people into zombies. That's a slander put out by another clinic in town that is being left in the dust as Dr. Richie takes off."

He paused, a bit taken aback by her vehemence. "It was just a joke," he said softly.

She changed immediately. "I'm sorry. I'm just a little touchy about it."

She settled back against him. "This exercise works better when the two are more evenly matched in size, but you can get the general idea. Raise your arms. Now sway with me."

He raised his arms and swayed.

"Calm your mind. Let your eyelids droop. Think of water lapping on the white sands of a tropical beach. Feel it lap. Feel the hot sun on your shoulders. Feel the gentle breeze ruffle your hair."

Little by little, he was feeling more than he'd expected to. As she moved against him, he became aware of just where her rounded bottom was touching his. It was incredibly arousing. The more she swayed, the more he forgot about the beach and focused on her body.

Sensation shot through his system and he held back an urge to make an appreciative noise. This was unbelievable. He'd been turned on by a woman's backside before, but not like this. This was overwhelming.

He was vaguely aware that she was still talking. He didn't need talking. He'd found that floating thing she'd mentioned and he was up there, drifting on a sensual cloud.

"Okay, now I'm going to lean my head back on your shoulder and you lean your head on my shoulder."

Whoa. He'd had sex that was less exciting than this. His heart was beating as though he'd just run a mile. Their heads were now side by side and the sense of her was flooding into his system. He turned his face toward her. He couldn't help himself.

She was saying, "Arms at shoulder height and straight out. Now turn the palms up," and he was breathing in her scent, filling his lungs with it and wondering what her mouth tasted like.

She glanced over, saw his face too close and hesitated. That was all he needed. He was going to kiss her. It was going to be a little odd, upside down and all, but he was going to do it. He made a move toward her and saw her eyes widen.

Whether they were widening with shock or interest he would never know. He would have liked to think the latter, but realistically, it wasn't likely. At the moment of reckoning, the door opened and a voice interrupted everything.

"What's going on here?"

Two

Abby was up and flying away from Daniel like a scalded cat. He would have looked twice, just to see how she could possibly have done that, but he was too busy taking the measure of the man in the doorway.

"Oh, Dr. Richie!" Abby was saying. "I'm just— We were just— Well, this is Daniel O'Callahan and he's just—"

Daniel hadn't really paid too much attention to the good doctor before, but now he looked him over and decided he didn't much care for what he saw. Dr. Richie was a tall, good-looking man, but there was something a little too polished, a little too calculated in his manner. His dark hair was salon-perfect and streaked with silver the way an actor would have had it done in an attempt to give gravitas to his appearance. That was it. Somehow the man looked like a performer to him. Something just didn't quite ring true.

And—let's face it—he didn't much like the way Abby was lapping him up with a spoon. Did she have to idolize the man?

Daniel rose slowly, just to make sure the doctor didn't think he was as embarrassed at being caught in this vaguely compromising position as Abby was.

"I didn't hire you to do this sort of training," Richie was saying to Abby, turned as though he thought he could carry on a conversation in private if he just didn't admit there was anyone else in the room. "We have counselors for that, Abby. I hired you to take charge of our public relations operation. You don't have time for this sort of work."

"I was just showing him. He was interested and I thought—"

Dr. Richie turned, acknowledging Daniel with a slight nod.

"I'm sorry, but I'm afraid you'll have to come to one of our seminars if you want to get a good overview of what we have to offer," he said, his attitude pleasant but distant. "And, Abby, I've called a senior staff meeting in the library. Please join us. The others are waiting." Another curt nod and he was on his way down the hall.

Daniel turned to look at Abby. Her cheeks were bright red in a very attractive way, but he regretted that she was taking this so badly.

"Sorry," he said. "Didn't mean to get you into trouble with the big boss."

She looked up at him but she didn't smile. He could tell she'd had it with him, and she was ready to let him know that.

"I'm afraid I'll have to ask you to leave," she said shortly.

"Okay," he said amiably. "But I'll be back when—"

"Out." Her dark eyes smoldered with anger and she pointed at the door. "And don't come back here."

With a shrug, he started toward the door. "I'll see you at the seminar tomorrow," he said, glancing back at her.

"Fine. But you won't be talking to me." She followed as though ready to shove him out into the hallway if he balked. "There is really no need for us to have any further communication. I'll make sure they assign a good counselor to you."

He stepped through the doorway and looked back.

"Someone who will be a good match for your needs," she added.

That stopped him cold. "My needs?"

"You know. That little problem you have." With a look of quiet triumph, she closed the door.

"Women!" Daniel said a few minutes later to his grandmother as he strode back into her hospital room. "Who needs them?"

"I'm a woman, darling." Phoebe looked up with a loving smile.

"Yeah, but you're sane. Not many other women can say that."

"Watch your tongue, young man," a tart voice stated, emanating from the tiny bathroom off to the side. "In the war between the sexes, I'm a major general." A woman about his grandmother's age emerged, carrying a vase full of roses.

Phoebe laughed. "Ella, meet Daniel O'Callahan, my grandson. Daniel, Ella Crown is the hospital florist and she has kindly delivered the flowers your brothers sent me."

Ella nodded but she didn't smile. Instead, she went on grumbling as she carried the vase to a shelf where Phoebe could have a good view of it. Her long white hair was twisted into a braided ring at the top of her head, and her naturally craggy face was enhanced by some of the brightest blue eye shadow he'd ever seen.

"So you're an expert on relationships, are you?" Daniel noted casually. "Then you might be the one who can explain to me why women are so perverse."

"I'm not explaining anything," she said, turning to fix him with a steady stare, her hands on her slender hips. "Why should I give secret intelligence to the enemy?"

Daniel grinned. She was a feisty one, and probably annoying as all get out in the long run, but he found her amusing. "Don't you want to make this a fair fight?" he asked.

"Heck no." She snorted. "Listen, youngster, I've married, harried and buried four men. I've done my part."

Daniel nodded, impressed. "Going for a fifth?" he asked her.

She practically snarled. "I think not. I've retired from those battles. Hung up my spurs. I think I've probably had more than my share of heartbreak. Why would I ask for any more punishment?"

"Oh, come on, Ella," Phoebe remonstrated, her eyes dancing. "You work every day with flowers, the language of love. How can you ignore the effect on you?"

"I keep my vaccinations up to date," she snapped back. "I'm not falling for any of this romantic twaddle. There's enough of that going on around here to choke a horse, anyway."

"You've noticed it, too?" Daniel said quickly. So few would admit it.

"Noticed it?" Ella rolled her eyes, an interesting movement backed as it was with the heavy blue eye shadow. "You can't get down the hall-

ways without tripping over lip-locked lovers
these days. I don't know what's come over
everyone."

That was a relief. He was beginning to think he
was the only one who saw the difference. The thing
was, he knew this hospital pretty well. His partner
had taken a round in his leg a few years ago, the
by-product of a major drug bust, and he'd visited
Jimmy almost every day until they'd let him out.
And there had been others—Minnie the office sec-
retary when she'd had her heart attack, Kirk with
his hip replacement, Mike with the broken back
from falling off a roof while chasing a kidnapper.
And then when Jimmy and his wife had decided
to adopt a child, he'd become well-acquainted with
Maggie Sullivan, a social worker with Children's
Connection, which was affiliated with the hospital. All in all, he'd been in and out of the place
dozens of times. If things had been like this he
would have noticed. It had only been this summer
that he had begun to notice people here acting
strangely. Only since the new clinic had opened its
doors.

So he nodded in agreement with the woman.

"I don't suppose you've visited the Healthy

Living Clinic by any chance?" he asked. "Or had any dealings with their products?"

"Heck no. I'm fit as a spring colt, thank you very much. I don't need any of that alfalfa-sprout mumbo-jumbo."

She started for the door, then glanced back at Phoebe. "You take care, honey. Enjoy your flowers." Looking back at Daniel she added, "And you take care of this little lady. Don't go running off after some flirty skirt and leaving her to fend for herself. You hear?"

Daniel put his hand over his heart. "On my honor," he told her earnestly.

She nodded as though satisfied and went on her way, her high heels clicking on the tiled floor.

Phoebe laughed. "Quite a character, isn't she? I've known her since we were in the Oregonian Historical Society together, years ago. I've even met a couple of her husbands."

"Sounds like you had to work fast to do that," Daniel noted. "None of them lasted very long." He looked thoughtful. "I wonder just what the circumstances were."

"Oh, no you don't!" Phoebe cried. "You leave Ella alone." She gave him a look of pure exasper-

ation—a look he'd seen many times before.
"She's a peach. Look, she stopped by the travel
bureau and picked up some brochures on cruises
for me." She waved the brightly colored leaflets
at him. "I've already got my cruise picked out."

Daniel stopped, groaning internally. "Gram, I
don't think you're going to be in any condition for
cruising for some time," he said carefully. "I hate
to see you get your hopes up when—"

"Don't start with me, young man."

He bit his tongue. There was no way she was
going on a cruise. It was impossible. The summer
had begun with her being hospitalized with circu-
latory problems, and then there had been the fall
she'd taken, an accident that had left her lying
helpless in the street. He couldn't bear to think of
her risking another accident like that. And even
if she were in physical shape to do it, the money
wasn't there.

He'd just sunk every penny in a wonderful retirement community for her. Now all he had to do
was convince her that she wanted to move in. But
there would be plenty of time for that once she
was back on her feet again.

"You just get over here and adjust these pillows

for me," she was saying. "Then you can turn on my television and go out and find a nice girl to date."

He obliged about the pillows right away. "That's just my complaint, you know," he said with a sad smile, meant to get her sympathy. "There are no nice girls left."

Phoebe looked up at him, her eyes narrowing speculatively. "That cute little redheaded nurse was asking about you again."

He threw out his hands in a mock gesture of irritation. "Now see, that's what I mean. That's just plain weird."

"Why?"

He shrugged, ready to pass her question by. But the way she was looking at him, he could tell she wasn't going to be satisfied with that, so he tried to explain. "Women just don't do things like that around me. I'm not that type of guy. Never have been."

"Oh, Danny, don't be so dense," his grandmother said crossly. "Women would love you if you just give them half a chance. And the redhead is the proof."

"No, Gram." He shook his head. This was one thing in his life that he didn't doubt. "There's something wrong here. Women have never fallen all over me like this before. And in such strange ways. I don't trust it."

"Oh, Danny."

"It's the truth. Women just don't act like that around me."

"Well, how do women usually act?"

He grimaced. "Most of the women I deal with these days reach for their license first, and then for their cell phone."

She looked bewildered. "Their cell phone?"

"To call their lawyer."

"Oh." She laughed. "Of course. They're afraid you're going to arrest them." She shook her head. "Well, very few here know you're a cop so that isn't the problem."

He slumped down into the chair beside her bed and squinted his eyes, thinking. "That's just it. It's driving me nuts. I've got to get to the bottom of it. I've got women making goo-goo eyes at me all over the place."

"Well, of course you do, darling." She patted his arm. "I think you just never noticed it before. You're quite a handsome man. I'm sure there are lots of women sizing you up as a very good catch. You just don't pay enough attention."

He gave his grandmother a patient look. "That's not it, Gram. I pay a lot of attention. It's part of my job to pay attention. And I've never been a ladies' man before." He sighed, mulling things over. "Anyway, it's not just me. Half the people in this hospital seem to be wandering around in a lovesick daze. You heard your friend Ella. She's noticed it, too. Something deeply suspicious is going on around here."

Phoebe still looked dubious, but she was lost in memories for the moment. "The trouble is, you don't take advantage of opportunities when they slap you right in the face. I remember that talkative Taffy Williams who used to come around to see you. She wasn't a beauty, but she seemed to be such a nice girl. You never did ask her out, though, did you?"

Daniel looked at her, considered for a moment, then decided to tell her the truth. "Gram, Taffy had a sex-change operation three years ago. She's now a he. You can stop trying to get me to ask her out. Uh, him out... Oh, hell!"

"My goodness. I'm sorry to hear that." She put

a finger to the side of her nose, thinking. "I must send her a get-well card."

Daniel laughed out loud. "You don't 'get well' from a sex change." He sobered. "At least, I don't think you do."

"Never mind. Everyone likes to get a card showing concern. Even if we're not too clear what that concern is all about." She smiled at him, then looked eager. "Now tell me. What is your investigation turning up?"

He turned to look at the wall. "Nothing so far."

"Danny! Don't hold out on me now. Tell me what's up."

He looked back at her. "Gram, I don't think you need to—"

"It has to do with that Healthy Living Clinic place, doesn't it?"

He reacted with surprise, then resignation. "How did you figure that out?"

Her smile was smug. "Where do you think you got your inquisitive genes? I heard what you said to Ella. That snapped it into place right away. So give."

"There's nothing to 'give,' you rascal." Leaning forward, he kissed her cheek with genuine affection. "I've been snooping around, but so far nothing looks even vaguely promising."

She pouted. "At least tell me what I can do to help."

He gazed at her, loving the way she wanted to get involved, but knowing it was something she just couldn't do. He would lay down his life for this woman who had stepped in and taken over when his parents had been killed in a boating accident. She'd been way past her most energetic years at the time. By all rights, she should have been spending her days having tea and cookies with her lady friends, joining the gardening club, taking tours of Europe. Instead, she'd pitched in and taken over parenting duties that had helped keep him and his three younger brothers together.

It had been no bed of roses for her, either. He and his brothers hadn't appreciated her at first, and they'd rebelled, each in his own way. As he looked back now, with the perspective of time, he could see that he had been emotionally devastated by the death of his parents, that he had taken it out on his grandmother, his community and, probably most of all, himself. There had been a time when it had been a toss-up as to which side of the law he would end up on. If it hadn't been for his grandmother, always a steady rock of love and understanding, he wasn't sure he would have made it back.

Oh, what the hell. If she wanted to help, there must be something he could think up to let her feel useful.

"Okay, here's what you can do. You can ask around about the Healthy Living Clinic. Just casually work it into the conversation. When nurses and therapists drop by, ask if they know anything about it, or if anything strange is going on there."

"What *is* going on there?" she asked in a stage whisper, her eyes huge.

He looked at her and hid his grin, answering her with the same sort of whisper. "That's what I'm trying to find out."

"Ah."

"It's not anything big or deep or dangerous. I don't think. I'm just curious."

"I see." She nodded wisely and gave him a little wink.

"No, Gram, I mean it. Just ask around. No big deal."

She stuck her nose in the air. "I know how to keep my cool, as we used to say in the jazz age."

"The jazz age." He laughed softly. "Okay, Gram, have your fun."

He sobered, realizing he might be unleashing a whirlwind.

"But under no circumstances are you to take any products from that place. No vitamins or tonics or lozenges. Don't do any of their exercises either."

He thought for a moment and added, "In fact, don't let any people from that place into your room. Okay?"

"You can trust me," she said stoutly.

"Good. Now can I trust you to get some rest?"

"Of course. Just turn the TV to my favorite soap and I'll be out like a light in no time."

If only he could believe it was really that easy.

He headed down the hallway toward the elevator, punching the button and looking up as the doors opened to reveal the very attractive redheaded nurse already ensconced.

He hesitated. There was something about the look in her eye that reminded him of a cat with a captured mouse.

"Come on in," she said, batting her eyelashes. "There's plenty of room."

He nodded to her warily and stepped into the opposite corner of the car. She immediately moved toward him, and as the doors closed again, she reached out and fingered the fabric of his suit coat.

"Nice," she said softly.

He frowned at her, unable to believe this. "You like this suit?" he said incredulously. It was off the rack at a discount store.

She smiled up at him seductively. "I like what's in it."

He stared at her, aghast. Now that just wasn't natural. Nice, but not natural. And when the doors opened again, he escaped as quickly as he could.

Abby was just passing through and she really didn't have time for this. That was what she told herself as she stepped lightly down the hall in search of Room 707.

She'd stopped by the nurses' station to pick up some reports and they had told her of a lady who wanted more information about the clinic. That wasn't really her function, but she didn't want to be rude. She supposed she could drop by and be friendly at least. If she could only find the room.

There it was.

She stuck her head in and found a little gray-haired woman dozing in her bed.

"Hi, there," she said brightly.

The woman looked up and smiled a welcome. "Hello."

"Are you Phoebe—" she glanced at the chart on the wall "—O'Callahan?" She turned and stared at the woman, suddenly remembering the O'Callahan she'd met the day before. Frowning, she decided there must be a lot of O'Callahans in the city. Funny coincidence, though.

"The nurse at the station told me you were asking about the Healthy Living Clinic, and since I'm spending some time on this floor, I thought I'd stop by and see if I can answer any of your questions. I'm the public relations representative."

Phoebe beamed. "Well, thank you, dear. Come right in."

Abby made her way to the side of the bed. "I wish I had some literature to give you, but we've recently revamped the brochure and new ones won't be available until later this evening. But I'll be sure to have some sent over for you."

"Isn't that nice of you." Phoebe gestured toward the chair. "In the meantime, you just come and sit right down here where I can look at you and you can tell me everything."

Abby laughed, pulling the chair over and dropping down into it. "Everything? Well, the clinic was started—"

"No, honey. That's not what I mean." Phoebe's eyes sparkled. "First off, are you married?"

"Married?" Abby was startled by the question. "Why, no."

"How nice. Got a fella in mind?"

"N-not really."

"Wonderful." She was grinning ear to ear. "Now tell me about your job. How did a nice girl like you get mixed up with that bunch?"

"Mrs. O'Callahan!"

"Call me Phoebe. And tell me what that good-looking Dr. Richie is really like."

Abby laughed. "Well…"

Half an hour later they were still chatting, though Abby was beginning to glance at her watch. She was just getting her things together and preparing to say goodbye when a figure appeared in the doorway. Looking up, her smile froze on her face.

Darn! This *was* the same O'Callahan after all.

The man had been plaguing her mind for the last day and a half. Whenever she got a moment of rest, his image came back to her and she found herself wondering what his visit to her office had been all about. His attitude had been so strange and his requests sort of oddball. She'd tried hard to accommodate him, to the point where Dr. Richie had thought he had to give her what she considered a humiliating reprimand. But now that she thought it over, she knew her employer was right, and she also knew that Daniel was someone she should avoid.

Now here he was again, looking tall and lean and somehow vaguely dangerous in a way she couldn't quite put her finger on. It was definitely time for her to take her leave.

Daniel was staring at her in surprise that quickly turned to suspicion. Again. What did the man instinctively have against her? It was so strange. People usually took her at face value, and her value was pretty high, if she did say so herself.

"What are you doing here?" he demanded.

Her chin rose. The man had a lot of nerve. "What are *you* doing here?" she countered.

He nodded toward Phoebe. "This is my grandmother."

That was too bad. She'd really liked the older woman a lot. Now she was going to have to be careful to avoid her.

"Well, that's something I guess the poor dear can't be cured of, isn't it?" she said, then recoiled, immediately wanting to bite her tongue for using such a sarcastic tone. But the man had asked for it.

"Children, children," Phoebe scolded. "I see you already know each other, so I won't introduce you. But I may have to give you a quick lecture on playing nicely with each other."

Abby turned apologetically and took Phoebe's hand. "I'm sorry. I didn't mean to disturb you. We've had such a nice talk and I hope we get a chance to do that again. But I'm overdue at work. I must get back. There's a staff meeting at eleven."

Daniel snorted. "Poor old Richie Strong is probably wandering the halls like a lost puppy, looking for you right now," he said.

Throwing him a poisonous look, Abby smiled at Phoebe. "I'll be back in the morning with those brochures."

"Ah, the famous brochures," Daniel said softly.

She blinked and forced herself to smile even more broadly. "What time does your grandson usually come to visit?" she asked Phoebe as she turned to go. "I want to be sure to miss him."

"I don't want you coming back here at all," Daniel said, his voice pleasant, but his eyes steely.

"Daniel!" Phoebe was outraged.

"I mean it, Gram. I don't want you dealing with stuff from that clinic. They've got some kind of voodoo vibe going on over there, and I don't want you involved."

"You are impossible," Abby said through clenched teeth.

Fury sizzled all through her system. She'd never before come across anyone who could instantly turn her usual complacency to rage the way this man did. Turning on her heel, she meant to make a dramatic exit. The only problem was, her first target seemed to be a closet. She realized her error immediately, but not soon enough to hide it from Daniel.

He grinned, standing in her way with his arms crossed.

"I'm beginning to understand where you make your mistakes," he told her, "and how you end up locked in places you shouldn't go into. You see, this is a door, but it's not the right door. This is a door to a closet. That is the door to the outside world. Not the same thing."

She knew her face was bright red, but right now she didn't care. She only wanted to get out of the room before she did something really stupid. Her hands were already balled into fists. What would he do if she took a swipe at his nose? Oh, was she ever tempted!

"Could you just please get out of my way?"

"Oh. Certainly." He stepped back, but at the same time, a crew began rolling another bed into the room and they both had to stand against the wall to let them pass and maneuver the bed.

"So what are you doing now?" he asked her softly, his words covered by the commotion in the room. "Trying to go after me through my grandmother?"

"Go after you!" Her jaw dropped and her hands itched to grab something to throw at his head. She had to suffice with glaring daggers at him. "Of all the egos I've ever known, yours is the most inflated. It's practically bouncing off the ceiling."

The pretty redheaded nurse had come into the room along with the moving crew. Abby noticed her distractedly as she handed Phoebe a cup with pills in it and turned to go, pausing to glance at the other two, deep in their argument.

"Well, I don't know," Daniel was saying in what Abby thought was a truly insolent manner. "Evidence isn't everything, but it sure can point in a direction and—"

"Evidence!" She jabbed her forefinger at his chest. "I'd say the evidence shows you were the one coming after me yesterday. Name one good reason why I would be going after you."

The nurse shook her head and grinned as she passed them. "Just check out those biceps, sweetie. They'll give you a clue."

Abby whirled and glared at the woman, but she was disappearing through the doorway.

Daniel grinned. "See? Why would I be going after you when I've got beautiful redheads following me around?"

"Oh!" She tried to leave but the crew was

wheeling the bed back out again. Something about a broken control button. So she contented herself with hissing at him out of the side of her mouth. "Just stay away from me, Mr. O'Callahan."

"Fine. And you stay away from my grandmother."

She turned her head so fast, her hair whipped around her face. "Your grandmother is a grown woman. She can have visits from any friends she wants."

He shook his head, looking exasperated. "Why are you always talking back?"

"You can only talk back to an authority figure. And I don't see one here."

A space opened up, and she finally made good her escape.

"See you tomorrow night at the seminar," he called after her, making it sound like a threat.

"Not if I see you first," she called back.

Something about the way she was stomping off made him think she would have liked to have his prone body under her shoes. He pictured that, and, for some reason, he was grinning again.

"Daniel O'Callahan, what are you doing treating that lovely young woman that way?" Phoebe demanded when they finally had the room to themselves again.

He looked at his grandmother and sighed, suddenly deflated. The thrill of the fight was wearing off, and he realized it hadn't gone as well as he might have thought at the time. Funny how that happened.

"I guess you could say that I just gave you a demonstration of why I don't date much," he admitted.

He thought for a moment of Charlene, the last woman he'd gone out with, and winced, trying to push that picture right out of his mind. That was one his grandmother didn't know about. Charlene was a stripper. With the mandatory heart of gold, he supposed. But still, a stripper.

That was the down side of being a cop. You spent so much time with the underside of life that was what you got used to, whom you felt comfortable with. And added to that, everybody started to look like crook.

Quite a contrast to Abby Edwards. She was Snow White compared to what he was used to. Not his sort at all. In fact, the very type he should stay away from, especially now when he was on administrative leave from his department.

He winced, wishing he could get over the bitterness. All his years of hard word and loyalty to the force seem to count for nothing once there was an accusation lodged against him. He knew the rules were the rules and this was the way things had to be. But that didn't mean he had to like it—especially since the charges were to transparently lame. A man he'd arrested later charged that he'd stolen a great deal of money from him during the arrest. The man just happened to be the brother of a prominent politician, so though there was no evidence at all against Daniel, he was on the hot seat and had to go through a complete investigation and a hearing. Did he feel betrayed? Hell yes!

And that only fed into his natural cynicism, making him feel even more like an outsider. And making him a very bad fit for a women like Abby.

So why was he looking forward to that seminar more than ever?

Three

Abby turned her back to her full-length mirror in the bedroom of the apartment she shared with a sleek black cat named Ming. Looking over her shoulder, she frowned at her own reflection in the glass. Was she getting fat?

Her mother's voice sounded in her head. "Now, Abigail, you stay away from mirrors. Looking at yourself too much will only bring on shallow thinking. There are more important things in the world than looking pretty."

She frowned, shaking her head. She'd listened

to her mother and avoided shallow thinking and spent her high school years winning all the awards but looking like a drowned cat most of the time. Thinking back now, she realized that a little more balance might have been useful.

"Just a little shallow thinking," she murmured to herself. "And not quite so much killing myself with homework and piano lessons and science club."

She'd made her parents proud as peacocks, but she hadn't had a date to the senior prom.

It had only been in the last few years that she had learned how to make herself look good. And her mother still didn't trust it. She grinned, thinking of her.

"Too bad, Mom," she muttered. "You've got Daddy. How am I supposed to get a man of my own if I don't do what has to be done to get one?"

At first she'd attacked a beauty regimen as a project to be mastered, just like she did everything. She was one of the few people in the world who studied hairstyles and lip gloss the way astronomers studied the stars. For a while, she was maniacal at self-improvement.

But that didn't last all that long. Very quickly

her intrinsic sense of proportion took over and she relaxed a bit. The natural look was more her mode anyway—as long as natural didn't mean unkempt and careless.

She'd seen a response in male interest right away and she'd actually dated a bit. But the men she'd met that way hadn't exactly rung her chimes. Nice men—but no violins, no flight to the moon on gossamer wings.

And yet, a yearning had begun to grow in her. And she had to admit, deep in her heart, that this was one of the reasons she'd gone after the job for Dr. Richie the way she had. She'd met him at a Chamber of Commerce meeting where she'd been gamely trying to drum up some business for her flagging public relations firm.

He'd been very friendly to her. In fact, he had a way of talking that had made her feel as though she was the only person in the room, the only person he cared about at all. It was sort of thrilling, actually, to have this famous media star act as though he was interested in her and her alone. She'd felt lighter than air that day.

She'd overheard him complaining about his PR team and she'd immediately begun to think about going after the job. It had helped a lot to re-store some of her wavering confidence when he'd seemed so impressed with her work.

"The man pretty much saved my life," she admitted to herself, reaching into the closet to pull out the blue silk suit she wanted to wear to the seminar. "Well, my professional life, anyway."

She paused, staring into space. Did that mean she had a..."thing" for Dr. Richie? She wasn't sure. For some crazy reason, Daniel O'Callahan flashed into her mind at exactly the moment she started to conjure up a picture of the good doctor.

"Ugh!"

She shook that image away. Why was that man cluttering up her brain? He was annoying, obnox-ious and just plain infuriating. And he seemed to take such pleasure in being a jerk.

Okay, so maybe he was sort of good-looking in a hard and dangerous way. And maybe he had made her laugh a time or two. Still, the way he always seemed to be looking for motives behind everything she did was downright offensive. She was going to avoid him like the plague from now on.

She slid the blue silk skirt up around her hips,

wondering why it seemed to be more of an effort than usual. And then the zipper stuck. Looking into the mirror, she noticed the way the fabric was pulling and groaned. She *was* gaining weight. And she was going to have to find something else to wear.

"Ming, I'm fat," she told her cat, who was busy laying down a carpet of black cat hairs in the middle of her white bedspread.

Ming looked up, narrowed her eyes critically, but didn't comment.

Tugging the skirt off, Abby began to look around for an alternative, and her gaze fell on the jar of NoWait, the new weight-reduction oil Dr. Richie had developed, sitting on her dresser.

She hesitated. Should she try it? Dr. Richie had given her a sample to use in order to get acquainted with the product and its effects, but she'd thought she might just pass on that. Still, it was true that she ought to know all about what she promoted. Maybe it was time to do exactly that.

She picked up the jar and curled her fingers around it. The feel was nice, hefty and smooth, and the look was inviting. Carefully, she twisted off the top. The scent that drifted up was fresh, a sort of musky citrus that had an exotic allure.

"Why not?" she murmured. Using her forefinger, she dabbed some behind one ear. It felt cool on her skin. She did the same behind the other ear, then closed the jar and looked at herself expectantly in the dresser mirror.

Well, what now? She didn't feel any different.

Shrugging, she turned to her closet to find something else to wear. Time would tell and she didn't have any of that left for lollygaging. The seminar was due to start in a little over an hour and she should really be there early to help set up.

A mint-green silk suit replaced the blue one. The skirt was a little snug, too, but not as bad as the other, and she was dressed and ready to go in no time.

"Wish me luck," she said to her cat as she pulled out her car keys and started for the garage. "I'm jumping into the deep end tonight."

Ming regarded her with a complete lack of interest in her golden eyes. In fact, she stretched out her leg and began cleaning it intently, just to prove she wasn't going to waste any more of her valuable time on someone who wasn't handing out food.

Abby laughed and opened the door. A balmy breeze was blowing, and something about it filled her with a sense of anticipation. Suddenly she was sure good things were coming her way tonight. As she walked toward her car, she found herself singing a silly love song, and she laughed again.

Life, it seemed, was exceptionally good.

An hour later Abby was at the microphone, getting the overflow crowd into the proper mood for Dr. Richie's speech. Expectations were running high. She could feel the energy behind all the faces turned up toward her, and it filled her with excitement. She wanted to know and touch every one of them. She'd never felt this way before— as though she were involved in something big, something important, something that had the potential to change a lot of lives. It was wonderful.

A ripple went through the crowd. She turned. Yes. Here he came, marching like a glorious champion, head high.

"Ladies and gentlemen," she said into the microphone. "Please welcome the man who has taken the Pacific Northwest fitness community by storm, Dr. Richard Strong."

Applause shook the rafters, rolling in waves as he walked, smiling and reaching out to take the hands that stretched toward him. Excitement grew as he emerged from the crowd and mounted the stage, taking the podium.

The consummate performer, she thought as she watched him, overwhelmed with affection and pride. He was perfect. Any woman would be lucky to end up with a man like him. She sighed as he looked over at her with an approving smile.

Any woman at all.

Daniel was standing in the shadows watching Abby and Dr. Richie interact. It was pretty depressing stuff. What did women see in the jerk, anyway? Did he have some sort of spell he cast over them? Looking around the room, seeing the fervent looks on some faces, he felt repelled more than anything else. Strange. He'd never understood the appeal of the man himself.

He did get the appeal of Abby, however. His gaze kept straying her way.

Her long shining hair hung down her back like a sweep of silk and her dark eyes looked huge in the stage lighting. She stood with her weight evenly balanced and her hips thrust a bit forward, making her look as if she was ready to dance at any moment. But most strikingly, her face was radiating happiness.

She looked, he decided, like someone at a revival who had just seen the light. He wasn't sure what it meant, but he was afraid a part of it was complete infatuation with the slick doctor at the podium. And that was enough to make him a little crazy.

Richie Strong was speaking and the crowd was drinking him in as though he held the secret to life.

"When actually," Daniel said to himself, "what he holds is the secret to hypnotizing a crowd."

You're jealous, a voice whispered in his ear. You're green with envy. You want to be the one Abby is sending those adoring looks to. Don't you?

He shrugged. Maybe. Just a little. But it never paid to be jealous of a media sensation.

From what he'd been able to glean from casual sources, Dr. Richie was the current star in the pantheon of fitness gurus who often burst upon the scene, spread their glory across the sky and burned out in a spectacular crash of raised hopes, or else faded away into obscurity as the people turned to someone else. Where had he come from? How had he arrived at this exalted status so quickly?

Those details were sketchy at best. It seemed he had suddenly appeared as a hugely popular motivational speaker, touting his fitness and lifestyle seminars all over the Pacific Northwest. Now he'd taken over the clinic here at Portland General and it was widely assumed he would use it as a base from which to launch an even more powerful enterprise. The man was the latest thing. The sky was the limit.

Why wouldn't Abby worship him? Everyone in the room seemed to feel the same way. From the looks he saw on their faces, they were all in the bag. Except for Daniel.

But that wasn't what he was here for. As he tuned in to the lecture, he found it more a sales pitch than anything else.

"No, my friends. This is not magic. Though you may think it is once you've experienced the speed and strength of the effects. My formula is based on sound scientific principles. There are certain immutable precepts in the foundation of nutritional studies. They are ageless and never change. What I have done is found a new way to work within the same framework that everyone else must work in. I've picked up on elements others have missed, made new combinations, seen things in a new light. And what I've come up with has proven to be one of the most exciting discoveries ever in the field of weight management. And that is what I have to share with you tonight."

"A hell of a lot of words saying basically nothing," Daniel murmured dispassionately, starting toward a chair in the back row that had suddenly opened up.

Unfortunately, a middle-aged blond woman had started toward the same chair at the same time and they collided.

"Oh. Sorry."

But instead of recoiling, the woman clung to his arm, searching his face.

"What was that you were saying?" she asked in a low voice, staring up at him.

He gave her a rueful smile. "I don't think I'd better repeat it," he said. "I might get lynched."

She nodded, biting her lip. "I thought I heard

you right," she whispered after someone shushed them both.

He gestured toward the chair. "You go ahead and take the seat. I'd rather stand anyway."

"No, no." She shook her head, looking toward the stage with sad blue eyes that struck him strongly. "You take it. I don't think I'll stay." She sighed, shaking her head. "I'm thinking of going out and getting myself a gallon of chocolate mint ice cream, anyway. And I plan to eat it very slowly."

They both pulled back into the shadows to get away from the angry looks.

"My name's Daniel O'Callahan," he said, offering his hand.

"Carrie Martin," she responded, shaking it and looking up at him with a direct gaze.

"I take it you're not here for the powerful weight maintenance program?" he said, curious about her. "Not under the spell?"

"The spell?"

"Of Dr. Richie."

She laughed shortly. "No. I may be a thick-headed, stubborn fool but I did learn my lesson. Too bad it had to be the hard way."

"So then, what are you here for?"

She looked at him for a long moment, almost as though weighing the consequences of telling him the truth. Then she punted, shrugging. "I'm just watching."

He shrugged, too. "So am I."

She sighed, looking back at the doctor at the podium. "I'm watching my past and throwing away my future," she murmured.

He didn't answer. He had a feeling that wasn't really meant for him to hear, and sure enough, she turned and began to wander away with only a slight smile over her shoulder in taking her leave. But he had a sense he would be seeing her again. She was the only other person in the room immune to the sales pitch. From what she'd said, he would assume that she knew something the rest didn't. That she'd actually had dealings with Dr. Richie in the past. And he had an even stronger intuition that she would provide him with some missing parts of the puzzle eventually.

He had an urge to follow her, try to get information out of her right now, but he resisted it. Some things had to be left to develop in their own time. Pushing too hard could ruin everything. He'd learned that by bitter experience time and time again.

He turned his attention back to the meeting at hand. Dr. Richie was still extolling the wonders of his new oil.

"Unwanted pounds seem to evaporate in just a few hours," he was saying. "Of course, a strict regimen of diet and exercise must accompany the use of the oil for any extended effects to be felt, but that becomes second nature once the results start coming in. You won't believe how easy it all becomes."

"The proverbial free lunch," Daniel murmured.

"Shhh," a large lady in a velour jumpsuit told him sternly.

"Sorry," he said, nodding his apology and reminding himself to keep his opinions quiet. You never knew what a room full of diet-crazed folk might be pushed to if they heard the truth. His wide mouth twisted into something resembling a smile. Snake oil was snake oil, no matter how pretty the package it came in.

"You have the power inside you," the voice from the front boomed, edged with a fine emotion now. "All you have to do is make the deci-

sion. Make it in your heart. And once that decision is made, be proud of it. Be ready to tell the
world."

Abby was going down along the side of the
room now and Daniel strained to see what she was
doing. Ah. She was passing out those brochures
she had been so sure would improve the image of
the Healthy Living Clinic. He stepped to the side,
placing himself right in her path, and when she
looked up and saw him he expected her eyes to
flash with anger, a continuation of the animosity
they seemed to strike so easily between them. In
fact, he was looking forward to it.

"Hi," he said softly, not wanting to be shushed
again. "Do I get one?"

She hesitated for another beat, her eyes wide
as she gazed into his. She looked prettier than
ever, her cheeks rosy with the intensity of the
evening, her eyes sparkling in the artificial light.
And suddenly, to his surprise, she smiled. Her
smile was large and genuine, white teeth flashing,
dimples twinkling.

"Of course," she said, handing him one. And
then she turned, starting down the next row.

He stood where he was, staring after her,

knocked silly. That smile had paralyzed him. He felt as if there was an anvil on his chest and suddenly realized he'd forgotten to breathe. Gulping in a quick hit of air, he got the lungs working again. But his gaze followed her up and down the aisles. He couldn't look away.

Wow. He'd never known a smile to make such a direct hit to his solar plexus before. And as he gathered his senses together again, he frowned fiercely, just to remind himself that he was a cold-hearted cop. None of this touchy-feely nonsense for him. He was made of sterner stuff.

Wasn't he?

Things were going great. Abby was walking on air. Everyone was so excited about the new program Dr. Richie had developed. She was really glad she'd joined the clinic and was working to promote such a great entrée to a healthy lifestyle for so many people.

"You're an angel," one woman told her, clutching her newly acquired jar of NoWait to her chest. "I thank you people with all my heart."

"You're an excellent candidate for this sort of

treatment, Mrs. Halliday," Abby told her earnestly, leaning against the counter set up at the back of the assembly room.

The place was crowded with people trying to get into the close circle around Dr. Richie, while those ready to go ahead and try the oil were lined up to see one of the two assistants signing clients to contracts. There were so many of these that Abby was handling the overflow.

"I know you'll do well. Now don't forget your schedule of appointments. We want to keep close watch on you, just to be sure your body is reacting as we expect it to. We don't take any chances with your health."

Mrs. Halliday toddled off and Abby looked up expectantly at the next person in line. When she saw Daniel O'Callahan standing there, she really wasn't surprised. For reasons she wasn't sure she wanted to analyze, she'd been expecting him.

"Oh, it's you."

Funny. She knew she'd been annoyed at him earlier. In fact, she vaguely remembered saying some pretty mean things to him. But right now she couldn't draw up any of that animosity, and she didn't want to anyway. She almost felt as though he was an old friend at this point. Someone she treasured.

Maybe it was because she was feeling so good about this job that it was spilling over into the rest of her life. She had a new attitude, as they said in the song. Her outlook had changed for the better.

Or maybe it was that he seemed different, too. Not quite so hard. Not quite so imposing. In fact, he looked sort of approachable with his soft white shirt under a light sports coat. And definitely hunk-like.

"Yeah. It's me." He didn't smile and his gaze was watchful. "The proverbial bad penny." He gave her a quizzical look, as though he didn't know quite what to expect from her and was ready to accept the worst. "So how are you tonight?"

She smiled, feeling warm and fuzzy all over. For whatever reason she'd pretty much decided there was something she very much liked about this man. "I'm really, really feeling good."

He nodded warily. "That's nice. You look like you're happy."

Like a woman in love.

The words flashed into his head but he shut

them out. They were words he didn't want to think or hear. He glanced at Dr. Richie and then back at Abby, wondering how far things had gone with these two. The rumors about the doctor and his casual way with women were almost as rampant as the tales of his successes as a great promoter. All in all he was the sort of man a smart woman like Abby should stay away from. Unfortunately, it was so often that very sort of man they seemed to flock to. He'd seen it over and over, in every walk of life. The scam artists prospered in all levels of society.

"*You* look really handsome tonight," she was saying, then she looked surprised, as though she hadn't realized she was prepared to say such a thing.

The remark startled him, too.

"No kidding?"

He frowned, studying her like a mystery that could be solved with enough effort. But maybe there was nothing strange here. Maybe she was playing him for a sucker. Maybe she was just setting him up for complete humiliation. Could be.

"So," he said carefully, watching her closely. "If you're planning to hit me, do it where it won't show, okay?" He raised an eyebrow, only half kidding. "That's the ticket. Leave no marks."

"Hit you?" She emitted a sudden, gurgling laugh. "Why would I hit you?"

He shook his head. "I don't know. Because you…sort of hate my guts, I guess. I mean, that was the impression I had. Earlier." He waited with a questioning look.

But she was waving away such a preposterous notion. "I don't hate anybody. That's just plain silly."

"Uh-huh." He was still searching her eyes for answers. "Call me silly, then, because I'm pretty sure I remember you warning me to stay away from you."

"And yet, here you are."

"Yeah, here I are."

Her unblinking gaze met his. "Why?"

"Why?" Yeah, why? It was a good question. "I guess because you smiled at me. Sort of threw me off my stride. I had to come over and find out what you're up to."

She produced those dimples again, smiling broadly. "Right now I'm 'up to' getting a drink."

Rising from her chair, she motioned for the people behind him to go back to the other lines.

There weren't many people left, so she didn't feel very guilty about it.

"They have tea and juice in the reception room. Want to come with me?"

"Why not?"

He walked beside her, but he was watching the knots of people still hanging around, most hoping to get a chance to speak to Dr. Richie. They were like groupies, for Pete's sake. He wanted to tell them all to grow up. Or at least start using their brains. How could so many people fall for this stuff?

"Quite a turnout," he mentioned as he stood back to let her pass through the doorway first.

"Yes, isn't it wonderful?" She was fairly shimmering with happiness.

"Great for the bottom line, I suppose," he said cynically.

"No." She turned and frowned at him, truly outraged by such a thought. "Great for the well-being of all who came. Great for the community. Surely you can see all the good that Dr. Richie is doing here."

"Oh. Of course." He managed to keep most of the sarcasm from leaking into his voice. "I've got a lot of respect for the guy." Respect for his ability to con a whole roomful of people—and one impressionable young woman.

But that answer seemed to satisfy her and she led him to the table where cups of punch were being poured. She finished off one cup and reached for another.

"I am so thirsty," she said. "Promoting healthy living can be dry work."

"No doubt." He took a few sips from his own cup, watching her over the rim. Hard to believe he'd found her a bit ordinary at first. Right now she was the prettiest thing he'd ever seen. He was going to have to remind himself often that she was a source, not a potential date. And he wasn't sure his "self" was going to listen.

"So did you match me up with a counselor yet?"

"What?" She looked blank for a moment, then remembered. "Oh, that. No. To tell you the truth, I didn't think you would show up tonight."

"Why not?"

She gave him a look. "Let's face it. You're not really the type. And it's obvious you don't have a weight problem. Tonight is all about the weight issue."

"So it seems to be."

She frowned, examining him in a new way. "So why *are* you here?"

He shrugged. He was used to supplying cover reasons for his activities. He did it all the time in his line of work. He'd been ready to do exactly that tonight. But now, face to face with Abby, he hated to add any more lies to the list he was working with.

"Just curious about what's going on," he said evasively.

Her eyes narrowed and she scanned him with earnest intensity. "No," she said. "That's not it at all."

He blinked. "Okay. But listen, I really enjoyed the presentation and—"

"Don't try to change the subject." She jabbed a finger at his chest. "I'll bet I can guess what your game is. You're an investigative journalist, aren't you? Are you with the paper? Doing a piece on us?"

He hesitated. Was that a good thing? She didn't look outraged by it. Maybe because she thought of Dr. Richie as a savior of mankind and didn't realize an investigative journalist would be digging up dirt about the guy. If there was any dirt in his background. Somehow he thought it was a good bet that there was.

She wouldn't like that. But she wouldn't like knowing he was with the Portland police department either. He was walking a line here. How much could he tell her?

"Well, not exactly," he said hesitantly. "But you might say I'm investigating the whole healthy living movement and—"

Her smile was triumphant. "I should have guessed. Of course." She leaned close and spoke in a hushed voice, as though realizing he had to maintain a cover in order to do his job. "You're doing a feature for a magazine, aren't you? What magazine is it?"

He grinned uncomfortably. "Look, I'm not at liberty to release the name of the organization I'm working for at this time. They're very strict about anonymity until we get the details nailed down."

She smiled happily. "I'll bet I can guess who it is. I've done an interview with *City Style* magazine before. That's the one, isn't it?"

He smiled and shrugged, knowing he was as good as lying to her but unable to think of any way around it at the moment.

She came even closer so she could speak more

softly, smiling up at him with a new excitement, so close that he could feel the heat from her body, smell the scent from her hair.

"Come on. You can tell me. Ask for anything. What do you want?"

For just a second, he thought the room had tilted. To his shock, he realized being this close to Abby was making him dizzy. Dizzy. What was it about this woman that did these strange things to him?

But she wanted to know what she could do for him and he was about to tell her. He had to be careful. With his head buzzing like this, there was a risk he might be a bit too explicit. What if he told her that she turned him on and he would like to get to know her better and explore the possibilities? He would never say anything like that. But what if he did?

It never happened. The woman behind him took that moment to stumble and try to catch her balance by throwing her hand into the middle of his back, jostling him forward and sending the juice in his cup right down the front of his snowy white shirt in a large purple splash.

He guessed now he had the perfect reason to talk to her again.

Four

"Oh!" Abby cried out.

"Hey," Daniel said, sucking in his breath as the cold juice hit his skin.

"I'm so sorry." The young woman who'd caused the accident apologized, but melted into the crowd as Abby tried to dab at the purple stain with napkins.

"That ain't gonna do it," a short, dumpy-looking elderly man told them both, shaking his head over the misbehavior of the young.

Abby looked up, distracted but unfailingly polite. "Oh, hello. Wilbur Mason, isn't it? Nice to see you."

"You better wash it fast or the shirt is ruined."

"He's right," Abby said despairingly.

Daniel looked down. He wanted to say it was no big deal. He wanted to laugh it off, say "forget it," but the stain was huge and it was ugly. Not to mention, cold.

"Let's go," Abby said impulsively, grabbing his hand. "I know what to do."

Her hand was warm and smooth and he let her lead him out of the room. Hell, he would have let her lead him anywhere. It was becoming that kind of evening. The dim light, the music piped in along the hallway, the scent of gardenias coming in from the courtyard, the look of her, the feel of her hand—everything was conspiring to put him fully in the mood for…a little close contact. And when you came right down to it he didn't get in that sort of mood all that often. He was usually too busy working.

Hey, that was okay. He was working here. Being with Abby was all part of the deal.

They made their way down one hallway and around a corner.

"I get it," he said cynically. "We're just going to walk around the building until the shirt dries on its own."

She threw him a look and laughed, then pointed out a women's restroom.

"In here," she said.

He balked, digging in his heels. "Whoa. I don't think so."

"Don't worry." She looked amused by his reticence. "This isn't the one we're using for the seminar. We're far enough away, I don't think anyone will come here. And just in case they do, I'll put out the 'out of order' sign."

Somehow that didn't give him a lot of comfort. "Haven't you got a men's room I could us?"

Her face scrunched up. "Sure, but I'd feel funny going in there with you."

"No kidding. Now you know how I feel."

"Oh, come on." She tugged on his hand. "No one will know."

"*I'll* know," he grumbled, but he took a deep breath, squared his shoulders and followed her inside. And looked around with eyebrows raised. "This is a restroom? It looks more like the lobby of a small hotel."

"See? This is the best place, believe me." She put the "out of order" sign on the door, just as she'd promised, then turned on the tap in one of the sinks.

"Take your shirt off," she said, turning back to him. "Here, I'll hold your jacket."

Slipping out of the sports coat, he handed it to her, then unbuttoned the shirt, took it off and tossed it into the water that was pooling in the sink.

"There you go," he said, turning back to face her.

"Oh!"

She was standing very still, staring at his torso, and she made a little sound that caused his heart to skip a beat. For the first time in his life he was more than just vaguely glad he had the kind of build that might bring on a sound like that.

He glanced in the mirror, noticed with a bit of surprise how the light gleamed on the rounded muscles of his shoulders and the hard panels and ridges that made up his chest. Well, yeah, it was a damn good bod if he did say so himself.

Abby certainly seemed to think so. She was staring at him as though she'd never seen a man without a shirt before. He had a moment of suspicion, wondering if she was putting on an act. She was a little old to be quite so seemingly naive and overwhelmed by a male body. As a cop, he suspected everyone and everything. But his distrust melted away quickly.

It wasn't that there was any proof that she was for real; it was more that he wanted her to be for real. So he was more than willing to give her the benefit of the doubt.

"Here," she said a bit shakily, handing him back his sports coat, blinking fast and swallowing hard. "You'd better put it on. You might get cold."

He took it from her but hesitated, fascinated by the wide-eyed way she was staring at him. "You okay?"

She raised her gaze to meet his and nodded. "You are so gorgeous," she said breathlessly. "Could I...?" She raised her hand. "Could I just touch you?" she asked softly.

That pounding he heard could have been someone trying to get in, but after a second or two he realized it was just his own heart beating out a primitive tattoo in his head as the blood began to race through his veins.

"Sure," he said, glad to hear that his voice didn't sound as choked as he'd expected. "Go ahead."

Her hand reached out tentatively, then settled just below where his collarbones met. It flattened out and began a slow trail down across his taut flesh.

"Oh!"

She made that sound again and he was instantly as aroused as he'd ever been. Grabbing her hand, he pressed it over his heart so she could feel the pulse. She closed her eyes, as if savoring it. He was beginning to lose rational thought. Another moment and he would be stepping over the boundary into pure animal instinct. Did he really want to do this?

Her face tilted up toward him and her lips parted and he decided kissing her was only going to be the first step. The sports coat fluttered to the floor and he kicked it out of the way, then pulled her up against him and lowered his head to take her mouth with his.

She opened to him as though she were giving him her soul, with no hesitation. She tasted sweet and hot and more exciting than the speed of a jet plane. The room was pulsing now, pulsing and throbbing and spinning—egging them on, driving home a rhythm meant to entice them into an ancient dance. He was ready. He felt as though he'd been born ready. Was she?

If not, she was giving a good imitation. Her body was melting against his, soft and warm and wonderful. He pressed harder so that she could feel how much he wanted her and she didn't pull away. That only made him hotter. All he wanted was to have her. Nothing else mattered anymore.

At first the sound of water running was just a part of it all, the river of existence, the lifeblood of the moment. It took the extra-loud splashing sound to remind them both of what they'd come here for.

"Oh!" Abby cried, jerking away. "The water!"

Water was pouring over the edge of the sink and making a mess. Daniel scooped up his sports coat, just saving it from a hungry stream, and Abby turned off the faucet, then grabbed paper towels and began mopping up the puddles, laughing all the while at this ridiculous situation.

Daniel watched her. He was breathing hard, but he was slowly regaining his equilibrium. As he did so, his brain came back online, and eventually, a thought came to him.

He was an idiot.

That thought began to hammer him insistently and he couldn't ignore it. What was he thinking? How could he be so dense?

Abby was mopping up the floor, then scrubbing at the stain in his shirt, and all the time she was chattering on and on about something. But he wasn't listening. His head was filled with a throbbing again, only not the good kind this time.

Logic, man. Where's that critical thinking you're so proud of?

Okay, you met Abby. She was a little put off by you from the beginning. She didn't exactly fall into your lap. You manipulated her a bit and she didn't like it. Then you got her in trouble with her boss and she really didn't like it. Finally, you spent a nice half hour trading insults with her in your grandmother's hospital room. You parted ways as you were thumbing noses at each other.

The next time you see her she's passing out brochures and tending to the needs of Dr. Richie. For some reason, she's suddenly your best friend. No, more than a friend. She's doing the eye thing, and smiling. She's become a different person. And worse, she's suddenly practically begging for love.

This was all wrong. With his training and his finely honed instincts, he should have seen it right away.

Abby had gone to the dark side.

Mentally he slapped his own forehead. Of course. Why did he notice it so quickly on others but take so long with her?

Because you wanted her new attraction to be for real. Sucker.

He swore softly, but Abby didn't notice. She held up the shirt.

"I can't get it out. You'll have to try stain remover."

"That's okay," he said gruffly, working hard at coming back to earth and steeling himself against falling into the Abby trap again. He should have known what it was from the first. He should have guessed that it would only be a matter of time before she'd succumb to whatever it was that was infecting everyone who had anything to do with Dr. Richie and his clinic. The love attack.

"Thanks for trying."

She turned and favored him with a glowing smile. Just a few minutes before, that smile would have had him panting like a puppy. But he was on to her now. He didn't even smile back. It was time he made another stab at being a professional.

"Tell me this, Abby," he said, shrugging back into the sports coat. "Have you been drinking?" He might as well eliminate any normal reasons why she might be acting so out of character.

"Nope. I don't."

He frowned. "You don't what?"

"Drink." She dazzled him with her smile again. "I never touch alcohol."

He nodded skeptically. "Right. Then you've been taking something."

She stared at him blankly. "What are you getting at?"

He hooked his thumbs in his belt and stared at her coolly. "I want to know what you're taking."

She frowned, shaking her head. "I'm not taking anything."

"Besides the clinic vitamins."

"Not even the vitamins. To tell you the truth, I

can't stand swallowing pills. So I don't take them."

He stared at her. She looked completely open. Would such a pretty face lie?

You bet.

Could he take her word for anything at all?

Not on your life.

But she claimed she hadn't taken anything.

Was he wrong? Was all this just a natural progression for her? He thought it over again, step by step.

Nah. No way.

She was acting like a girl with a crush—but earlier in the evening he could have sworn her crush was on Dr. Richie. As far as he could see, that meant she was as far gone as all the other love zombies he'd seen haunting the hospital halls.

"So I guess we're down to looking for pods in the clinic basement, huh?" he said grimly.

"Basement?" She was beginning to look perplexed. "I don't think there is a basement."

"Oh, there's a basement all right," he said knowingly. "If only in your mind."

She shook her head. "You're talking crazy." Her puzzled look faded and she smiled again.

"But you're awful cute." She sighed and looked down at the soggy shirt. "Why don't we go back to my apartment? I'll see if I've got the right kind of stain remover. I just can't stand to leave your shirt this way."

He hesitated, considering. Why not? It would be one more chance to see if he could figure out what she was taking. Because she had to be taking something. Unless the good doctor was in to some sort of remote mind control. Daniel couldn't actually rule it out, but he was pretty sure the chances were slim.

"Okay," he said. "Let's go."

Abby wanted to stop by the reception hall to let the others know she was leaving. Dr. Richie was still surrounded by fans, so she checked on the two assistants and told them, then stopped by the counter to pick up her things.

At each stop she looked back at where Daniel was waiting for her, and each time she did, her breath caught in her throat. He gave her chills, he was so sexy, standing there with his jacket hanging open, revealing that iron-hard chest with its lovely tanned ridges.

Janet Greco, one of the women she'd signed up for the NoWait treatment program that evening, noticed, too.

"Oh, my," she said appreciatively. "Is he yours?"

Abby felt as though she was glowing. "For the moment."

Janet sighed. "Where can I get one like that?"

Abby looked at him and her heart skipped a beat. He really was gorgeous. She slowly shook her head.

"I don't know. I think he's one of a kind. Sorry."

She was doing that floating thing again. She wasn't sure what it was, but she felt as though she were living on two levels at the same time. It was interesting that Daniel had asked her if she was drinking, because she felt like what she'd imagined it'd be like if she was drunk. Only not really. In fact, she didn't think she'd ever felt quite like this before.

Still, the duality was fascinating. There was the old, sober and sensible Abby on one level, watching all that was going on, and then there was the new bubbly Abby having a lovely time and feeling a deep, abiding love for all of mankind. And an especially deep and interesting attraction for one Daniel O'Callahan. She wanted to be with him, to talk to him, to kiss him again. She was beginning to think she might just be crazy about the man.

This had never happened to her before. She'd dated, had even liked a few of the men she went out with. But she'd never had that sense of having found that special one before. Hearing other women talk about falling in love had always left her feeling a little out of it. She'd begun to wonder if she'd just been born without the love gene or something.

And now it looked as though she might have found out she had one after all. If it had finally happened to her, she was glad it was with Daniel. He was strong and compelling and hunky as all get out. And he could kiss like nothing she'd ever dreamed of. Sighing happily, she went back to meet him.

Daniel followed Abby into her apartment, his best investigative antennae on the alert. It was a nice place, very much as he would have expected.

The furniture was casually modern. Books filled the shelves. A Lichtenstein reproduction decorated one wall, an original picture of two small children eating ice cream cones was placed on another. A large Armani porcelain figure of a 1920s flapper filled one corner of the room.

"Nice," he said, gesturing toward the fashionably dressed statue.

Abby smiled. "A gift from my parents when I finished my master's thesis."

He turned to look at her. He'd assumed she was well educated but he didn't know much more about it. "What was your subject?" he asked.

"The applications of transcendental meditation on modern psychological modes of auditory perception."

He grimaced. "No wonder they gave you an award. It was enough just to memorize a mouthful of a title like that."

"My parents always gave me awards for goals challenged and met. It was their way of motivating me."

He cast a cynical look her way. "Was all that really necessary? You seem pretty self-motivated to me."

She stopped what she was doing and looked back at him. "Thanks for noticing," she said quietly, smiled and went back to filling a kettle with water.

"Are you hungry?" she asked him. "I can whip up an omelet in no time."

He hesitated, tempted. He really was hungry. But he'd probably better not eat anything here. The last thing he wanted was to accidentally take the mystery substance, whatever it was.

"No, thanks," he said, wandering through her kitchen, trying to seem merely restless as he took in everything he could manage, trying to find something that could be the catalyst of the odd behavior she was exhibiting. "But you go ahead."

"Oh, no," she said with obvious regret. "I can't eat anything."

"Why not?"

"I'm on a diet." Pulling off the jacket of her suit, she made a slow pirouette before him. "Tell me the truth. Do you think I'm fat?"

The thin lacy shell didn't hide much and the shape of her full breasts just happened to be the sort of shape he liked the best. He winced, forcing back the natural reaction that tried to start up his libido again. There was to be no more lusting in this relationship. He had to remain completely detached and totally professional.

Still, he had to admit she had certain attributes that were bound to linger in his memory for quite some time.

"Fat? Oh, no." There could be no mistaking the honesty in his tone. "You're just right."

She pouted provocatively, looking up at him. "I'm fat," she insisted.

Either he was going crazy or she wanted more than reassurance. She was yearning toward him, aching for him, and it was all there in her eyes. Wasn't it?

His mouth was going dry. "You're crazy." He turned away, hands shoved into his pockets to keep from reaching for her. "You should eat something."

She sighed, and he wasn't sure if it was with disappointment that he obviously wasn't going to take her nonverbal invitations for some light intimacy, or if it was just with hunger.

"I might as well see if I can get this stain out," she said. "Keep an eye on the teakettle, okay? I'll just go down to the laundry room at the end of the hall. I'll be right back."

He waited until she was out of sight, then went into action. Working quickly, he opened cabinets one after another, then the refrigerator, looking for anything that might constitute a substance to bring on this lovesick fog thing. Nothing jumped out at him. He hesitated over a small piece of cake on a plate in the refrigerator. It had obviously been nibbled on. Something about it reminded him of Alice in Wonderland and he shrugged. Why not? He pulled a small evidence bag from the stash he always kept in his pocket and broke off a piece to take to the lab.

The water came to a boil and he poured it out into the waiting teapot, then stepped quickly to the bathroom, doing a fast raid of the medicine cabinet and taking two more samples, though he didn't hold out much hope for either one.

"I think this new spray I bought is doing the job."

Abby's voice came to him from down the hall. Surprisingly, it stopped him cold.

"That's great," he called back.

He looked down at the sample bag in his hand and for just a moment he felt guilty. He was snooping around behind her back. This wasn't a good thing.

But it was a necessary thing. And a part of his job. After all, the investigation had come first. His friendship with Abby was a by-product of the research he was doing.

What the hell was wrong with him? Just get on with it.

He set his jaw. One more room to check and he didn't have much time.

Her bedroom was dark. All he needed was one quick look at what she had on her dresser, and then he would be back out in the living room, acting innocent. Reaching around the corner, he didn't feel a light switch. He took a couple of steps into the darkness, reaching out to try to make contact with a toggle or a dimmer switch, judging just about where he would think one would have to be.

But instead of the wall, his hand came in contact with something furry. He saw a pair of golden eyes at the same time he heard the high-pitched screech as something came hurtling at his head.

"Hey!" he yelled out, batting it away, and something dark went scuttling from the room.

"Daniel?" Abby was coming down the hallway. "What's wrong?"

He got out of the bedroom in time, but he couldn't hide the scratch across his cheek.

"What have you got in here? A tiger?" he demanded, wiping a line of blood from the wound.

"Oh, no!" she cried.

He looked up pathetically, expecting sympathy and coddling, but Abby was rushing right past him into the living room, searching for the animal.

"Ming! Are you okay?"

She found the cat behind the couch and pulled her out, petting her and cooing. He knew it was a petty thing, but the fact that her first concern was for the cat really annoyed him. Especially when he could have sworn that cat was looking at him smugly over her shoulder.

"How many people keep an attack cat in their apartment?" he asked grumpily, dabbing at the wound with a tissue as he came in and sat down in an armchair.

"You scared her."

"She leaped at me out of the dark. I had to defend myself."

"Oh. You are bleeding, aren't you?"

She finally realized, did she? He was gratified to see a look of sympathy on her face. About time.

"Ming is sorry," she said, her tone just a touch sarcastic. "Aren't you, kitty? It would be a shame to have that handsome face all scratched up."

Putting the cat down, she went to the kitchen cupboard and took down a bottle of disinfectant, reaching for cotton balls at the same time.

He stared after her, startled. For just a moment there, she sounded like her old self, as though the love bug had worn off.

But as she dabbed at his wound, she chatted cheerfully, intimately, giving him looks that left no doubt as to where her emotions lay. Maybe he'd imagined it. Or maybe she just loved her cat so much, mere romance couldn't meet the standard set there.

"Come on," she said when she was done. "I'll pour you a cup of tea." She sighed. "If I wasn't on a diet, I'd add some cookies to the menu for good measure."

He followed her back into the kitchen, enjoying the way she seemed to fling herself about in the room, casually competent, supremely at home. There didn't seem to be any self-consciousness about her as she worked under his gaze.

"Maybe that's your problem," he said, just to

say something. "Maybe you're light-headed from lack of food."

She turned back toward him, frowning. "I didn't know I *had* a problem."

"Oh, you've got a problem all right." He grinned at her.

"And what is that problem?" she asked, hands on her hips.

He raised one eyebrow. "Me," he said softly.

He held her gaze with his. Something quivered in her, vibrating like a tuning fork. He wanted to kiss her again. All he had to do was reach for her. She wanted him to.

But he held back. A slight furrow remained between her brows. She was wondering why.

So was he. Deliberately, he pulled his gaze away from hers.

"I really ought to get going," he said abruptly.

She was shaking her head. "Can't."

"Why not?"

"Your shirt is drying. You'll have to wait."

He supposed she had him there. He grimaced. Oh, well, he'd tried to do the right thing.

"And anyway, the tea is ready. Sit down and have some with me."

He looked toward the teapot. He'd watched every move. She'd used nothing but commercial tea bags, sealed in their packets. He supposed he might risk having some.

"You can't exist on tea alone," he noted, still trying to dig into what she'd been putting into her system. "Especially when you won't take vitamins."

She turned back to the counter and began pouring out the tea into stoneware mugs.

"Oh, what do you know about it?" she said lightly. "I'll bet your eating habits are horrible."

He nodded slowly. He had to agree with her there.

"For instance," she went on, turning to hand him a steaming mug, "what did you have for breakfast this morning?"

He stopped, his back against the counter. He didn't have to think hard. This morning had been like every other morning. "Nothing."

She put her hands on her hips, making her breasts press against the fabric of her lacy shell in a way that made him swallow hard.

"And what did you have for lunch?"

He thought for a moment. "A cold beer."

"And?"

He shrugged, giving her a rueful grin. "That was it."

"Ahh."

"That was all that was in my refrigerator." He was teasing her now. "Beer is liquid bread, after all. Very nutritious."

"Dream on!"

"Wait. I did have something else."

"What?"

"I found an old Twinkie left over from—"

"Ugh! You are in sad shape." She picked up a packaged bar from a sack on the counter and handed it to him. "You've got to eat this right now."

He turned it in his hand. "What is it?"

"A nutritional bar. From the new clinic line."

He looked up sharply. "I thought you told me there were no products like this."

She shrugged innocently. "I hadn't heard about these. They're brand-new. We haven't even worked out the marketing for them yet."

His fingers tightened around it. Interesting. He looked at her out of the corner of his eye. "But you've been testing them."

"Sure. They've been testing them for the last few weeks."

Very interesting. This could be it.

"Uh-huh. Sure, I'll take one." He dropped it into his pocket. "I'll have it later."

"Good." She smiled at him. "Then you can let me know what you think."

"What? You haven't tried them?" Did that mean this theory was down the drain? He felt a definite letdown.

But she gave him a slight reprieve. "I haven't tried *that* flavor. The only one I've had is the peanut butter and chocolate chip."

"Oh." He relaxed. "Okay. I'll test it out and let you know."

"Why won't you try it right now?"

"Can't be done." He shook his head, looking wisely at her. "I never mix tea with nutritional bars."

She gave him an exasperated look, but didn't urge him any more. They took their tea to the living room and sat on the couch drinking and talking softly for the next half hour. Daniel sat in one corner and Abby curled up at the other end, her feet tucked under her. The sound of the dryer could be heard in the distance. Ming peered out from behind a chair, keeping an eye on Daniel, her golden eyes unblinking.

And Daniel talked about anything he could think of to keep from looking over at where Abby sat looking cute and inviting and definitely under the influence of something unnatural.

Watching Daniel slowly sip his tea, Abby had an overwhelming urge to start kissing his neck. It looked so good, the skin so smooth and golden against the rougher texture of the suit coat. She didn't dare let herself look at his chest too often. Who knew what she might get the urge to do there? It took her breath away.

She closed her eyes for a moment, truly shocked at herself. She didn't do things like this, didn't think these sorts of thoughts. But the impulse was there, and she couldn't deny it.

And what was wrong with him, anyway? A surge of annoyance swept through her. She'd set the scene. The lights were low. She had light jazz playing softly on the stereo. A cinnamon-scented candle was flickering on the coffee table, throwing intriguing sparkles of light around the room.

She'd given him pearl-essence tea, which the health food store guy had assured her had properties important in the art of seduction. She'd laughed at the time, sure she would never need it for that. But now here she was.

And…nothing.

The man could have been sipping tea with his maiden aunt. He was spending a lot of time staring at the far wall and he was talking on and on about some pirate movie he'd seen. This was not what she would have imagined an evening with the two of them sitting on a couch could be.

She had to do something to pull him out of ignore mode. It was too bad she didn't have more experience at seducing a man. In fact, she'd never tried it before.

But this was different from all the other times in the past that she had liked a man and never had the nerve to do anything about it. She didn't want to let this one slip through her fingers. She was just going to have to follow her own instincts, such as they were. Slowly, she stretched out one leg until she could nudge him with her bare foot.

He looked up, startled.

"I think it's time," she said softly.

He blinked at her. "Time for what?"

She smiled at him. "For you to kiss me again."

His gaze shifted uneasily. "I don't dare try that. Your cat is still on guard, you know."

"She won't hurt you."

"I never knew a cat yet who would follow orders."

She prodded him with her foot again. "I'll protect you, then."

He looked at her for a long moment. She was sure he was going to move toward her. But he did something odd instead. He winced, as though he was forcing himself to do something he didn't want to do, and he looked away again.

"Forget it, Abby," he said roughly. "You don't want to go kissing a guy like me. There's no future in it."

Future! What was he talking about? The future could take care of itself.

"Guys like you are the only kind worth kissing," she said lightly, hoping he didn't detect her disappointment. It would have been nice if he'd looked a little more interested. Instead, she got the feeling he was looking toward the door, wishing it would open and give him an escape route.

Ordinarily that would have been the end of it for her. She never pushed into situations where she wasn't wanted. But for some reason she couldn't let it go tonight. She couldn't really believe he didn't feel any attraction. Not after the way he'd kissed her earlier that evening. Just thinking of it made her breath come a little faster. Nobody else's kiss had ever had that effect on her.

"Abby, you deserve a man who will treat you right. A man who has a future for you. Someone who has your type of background and your type of friends and—"

"Maybe you're right," she broke in. If she let him go on, he would be putting her on a pedestal so high she was bound to break a leg falling off. "Maybe I do deserve some fabulous mythical paragon of excellence."

Uncoiling from her comfortable place at the end of the couch, she began to move toward him.

"But I don't want that, Daniel O'Callahan." She touched his cheek and smiled into his eyes. "I want you."

"You want me." He echoed her words mindlessly, grabbing her hand and pulling it away.

"No, Abby. Listen, you're crazy. You don't really want me. You want some nice guy who will treat you nice and take you to the country club and play tennis and do what's right. I'm not like that. I work the streets where things get ugly. I hang out with people you wouldn't let in your front door. I'm used to having things a little rough, a little dirty."

Something was quivering deep inside her. He was making her absolutely insane with wanting him.

"You seem okay to me."

He swore softly, turning his shoulder as though to stop her from coming closer and his eyes looked very dark. "Abby, I'm barely housebroken. I don't belong with a nice girl like you."

She pulled her hand back and placed it on his bare chest, spreading the fingers against his smooth, hard flesh and gasping softly at the feel of him.

"Why don't you shut up and kiss me?" she murmured breathlessly.

He hesitated. He was still going to try to get out of it. So she took matters into her own hands— literally—wrapping her arms around his neck and pulling him down until she was rewarded with a shuddering groan that seemed to come from deep inside him and his mouth took hers.

The room faded. Reality lost all importance. The only thing that seemed to matter was the sweet, hot taste of his tongue, the feel of his hands on her skin, the way her body was responding to his, as though she'd found a new world, a new state of being, and she never wanted to leave it again. He smelled so good, felt so smooth and hard, she was on a long slide to something new and she was ready to go.

But it all crumbled quickly, and he jerked away from her, rising and looking down at her, his green eyes a bit wild. He ran a hand through his hair, shaking his head, breathing hard.

"Okay, that's all," he said. "I'm getting out of here. If the shirt's still wet, I'll wear it anyway."

She looked up at him, feeling cold without his touch, not sure what he meant. "But—"

He shook his forefinger at her. "No more out of you. I know where all this passion is coming from."

She blinked, trying to clear her head. She was still fuzzy from his kiss. Maybe she always would be.

"You do?" she said, wishing she knew what the heck he was talking about.

"I do."

She frowned. "No, you don't."

He held up his hand. "Save it for the funny papers, lady. I've got your number and I'm already gone."

She sat where she was, frowning in bewilderment as he made his way down the hall and came back, his shirt hugging that wonderful chest.

"Thanks for the tea," he said, avoiding her gaze. "And for washing my shirt. I'll see you later."

"Alligator," she whispered dreamily.

He glanced at her once, hesitated, then shook his head and made his way out the door. "Good night," he called back. And then the door closed with a solid sound that seemed to seal a bad bargain.

She sat for a moment wishing she understood why he'd felt he had to leave. She was so disappointed. She'd finally found a man she could fall for and he was trying to avoid her. Closing her eyes, she called up the kiss again. That had been pretty spectacular. No doubt about it, that kiss was going to keep her warm for a long, long time.

Five

Daniel paced restlessly in front of the hospital entrance, looking up at the rain clouds gathering and waiting for his old partner. Jimmy had promised to drop by and pick up the samples he'd prepared to be tested at the lab. The answer to the mystery could be right there in the brown paper bag he held. He would know soon enough.

"Hey there, handsome."

He turned at the sound of the woman's voice, instinctively going into a subtly defensive posture. It was the redheaded nurse whose name, he'd heard from his grandmother, was Arline. He relaxed, but only a little.

"Morning," he said gruffly.

"You waiting for me?" she said with an impudent smile. "Or am I out of luck again?"

He hesitated. He didn't like this. If he thought she was just bantering, he could banter right back. But he was pretty sure she'd been love-bombed so she was basically a walking robot of flirtatiousness and not to be taken seriously. Just like Abby had been last night. How was he supposed to handle women like this? It was creepy.

"I do have something I wanted to ask you," he said, avoiding her question. "Have you been doing anything with the new Healthy Living Clinic?" As if it weren't obvious.

"Sure." She bobbed her head. "Dr. Richie is a genius."

"So I've heard. Listen, what kind of therapies are you into?"

She grinned, curling a strand of her long red hair around her finger. "I'm open to suggestion," she said teasingly. "What do you have in mind?"

"I'm talking about things at the clinic," he said, ignoring the implications in her flirtatiousness. "What are you taking? Anything besides the vitamins?"

A cloud came over her face and she lost the love look. "That is between me and Dr. Richie."

Daniel sighed with exasperation. He was losing patience with this case. He'd heard this evasive answer before. What was with the guy? Did he coach these people to make these slippery answers? If so, that seemed even more damning.

"Look, I'm just wondering because, uh, I was thinking about losing some weight, getting in better shape."

"Oh, sure." She grinned again, humor dancing in her eyes. "What are you *really* doing?" She wrinkled her nose. "You're already in great shape, from what I've heard. They say you were very macho with the open jacket and no-shirt look at the seminar the other night."

He groaned silently. "Where did you hear about that?"

"It's all over the hospital." She sighed with a longing that made him wince. "I only wish I'd been there."

"So you don't go to the seminars anymore?"

"No." She shook her head. "Actually, I think

I've lost all the weight I need to right now." She struck a pose that showed off her generous attributes to a fault. "What do you think?"

"I think too many woman are asking me to judge whether they're fat or not," he muttered, frowning. But he had to admit the truth. "You look pretty good to me."

"Really?" She sparkled. "Thanks. And just for that, I'll tell you what worked best for me."

"Okay. Shoot."

She leaned close and whispered it. "The atomizer. It changed my life."

"The atomizer?" He stared at her, bewildered. "What atomizer?"

She shook her head teasingly. "That's it. I'm not telling any more. You'll have to date me to find out anything else."

Before he could answer, Jimmy came striding toward the entrance and he didn't have time to quiz her further.

"Hey, Danny boy," Jimmy said in his usual friendly manner. Tall and dark, he was as handsome as they came, the sort of man who turned women's heads.

Arline looked once, then twice, then turned

her considerable charms his way and Jimmy's eyes widened.

"Well, hello, gorgeous," she said provocatively. "Where've you been all my life?"

If Daniel had any doubts about how quickly the love-struck of Portland General Hospital could transfer their affections from one love interest to another, he got the proof of it just watching Arline go after Jimmy. It made him laugh.

But then he thought about Abby, and that wasn't so funny. There was no doubt in his mind that her sudden interest in him was artificially produced by something from the clinic. And once she quit taking whatever it was that she was taking, she would back away from him as fast as she could. And that thought put him in a very gloomy mood.

"Sorry, darlin'," Daniel said once he'd seen enough. "Jimmy's married." Grabbing his friend's arm and beginning to pull him away, he looked back and said, "Say bye-bye, Arline."

"And go find yourself another victim," he muttered for only Jimmy to hear.

"Hey, she's pretty cute," Jimmy said, looking a bit woebegone.

"And you'll be pretty dead if Nadine finds out

you've been flirting with her," he said, mentioning Jimmy's wife.

"Nadine who?" Jimmy said, but he was laughing. Then he sobered abruptly. "You won't tell her, will you?"

"Nothing to tell," Daniel said with a smile. "Here are the samples I told you about. Let me know what you find out."

Jimmy took the bag from him. "Will do. Hey, the captain was asking about you yesterday."

"Oh, yeah?"

"Yeah. I told him you were doing okay."

"Oh, yeah. I'm doing great."

As great as a cop on administrative leave and under suspicion for something he didn't do could be doing. If he stopped to think about all the years of dedicated service he'd given to the department, only to be treated as though he was guilty the first time someone accused him of wrongdoing... Well, that was one reason he was pursuing this hospital mystery, so he wouldn't have a lot of time to think about it.

Jimmy hesitated, obviously noting the bitterness in Daniel's voice. "Well, okay. I'll call you when I know anything."

"Okay. And, Jimmy..." Daniel gave him a crooked half grin. "Thanks. I really appreciate it."

Jimmy's smile was open and genuine. "Any time, buddy. Any time."

Daniel went back into the hospital and took the elevator to the floor where his grandmother was. He got off just in time to see Ella Crown pushing her way past an older man he thought he recognized from the other night at the seminar.

"Don't you get in my way, old man," she was saying crossly. "I don't have any time for your shenanigans."

"Come on, Ella. Give us a little kiss why doncha?"

"Wilbur Mason, you keep your kisses to yourself. I don't need 'em." And she stomped off toward the elevator, leaving Wilbur behind looking dejected.

Daniel had to grin. It was a cinch Ella hadn't been delving into the secrets Dr. Richie had to offer. But from the looks of things, she was about the only one.

He turned into his grandmother's room and found himself face to face with Abby, who was sitting in a chair beside the bed. She looked up and favored him with a smile so warm, he felt instant sunburn.

He stopped dead. Didn't Abby remember what had happened the night of the seminar? There was no hint of it in her smile.

And here she was, dressed in a pink that gave her a cuddly, inviting aura, making her round places look even rounder and her soft places look even softer. It was as though someone had taken what tempted him most and added a decorative wrap guaranteed to add to the temptation. A cunningly baited trap if he ever saw one. He might as well go home and drink himself to death. It was all over.

"Good morning," she said brightly. "I brought Phoebe those brochures I promised her. And I've just been telling her all about what a success the seminar was the other night."

He looked from one woman to the other. Tight as two peas in a pod. What was this, a conspiracy?

"And I was telling Abby about the cruise I'm going on next month," Phoebe chimed in. "I'm so excited. It's been ten years since I've been on the *Northbound Queen*, sliding past those icy cliffs in Alaska. I can hardly wait."

His heart sank as he dropped down into the second chair. It was more than a conspiracy; it was doom breathing down his neck. How could she be getting her hopes up this way when it was clearly impossible for her to go on a cruise? She wasn't as sure on her feet as she used to be. There was no way he could let her take off on a ship all by herself, especially after spending all this time in a bed in the hospital. Didn't she see that?

And then there was the money situation. And his suspension from the force, making everything worse.

"Howard and I used to love the cruises," she was telling Abby, talking about her late husband. "You can't imagine how much fun it is. All that delicious food. The sea air. The fabulous shows at night. It all takes you away to a different world. Made us feel like royalty."

"It sounds wonderful," Abby agreed rather distractedly. Her attention was focused on Daniel and she couldn't hide it. She turned to look at him.

"So," she asked, looking at him archly, "what did you have for breakfast?"

He leaned back in his chair, his long legs out in front of him, and he stared at her, nonplussed. So she did remember some things about that night. That was a relief, he supposed. At least she wasn't blanking out on reality totally.

"Hey, I've got a perfectly good grandmother to ask me questions like that," he said gruffly. "I don't need nagging in stereo."

Abby looked shocked but he could see she was exaggerating for effect. Her eyes were sparkling with laughter. He was going to have to work very hard at keeping his distance today. Every time he looked at her, he could almost taste her again.

"You call that nagging?" she said. "Oh, brother. You obviously have never had much experience with the real thing."

"And I suppose you have?"

"You bet I have." She laughed, throwing back her head in a way that made him want to grab her and kiss her like crazy. "My parents are champs at it. Olympic level. Gold medal shoo-ins."

He gave her a skeptical look. "Just because

you've learned from the best doesn't give you carte blanche to try out your skills on me."

Their eyes met and immediately parted again.

"Well, I didn't mean to nag," she said a bit defensively. "But I am concerned that you start eating better. You can't run on those good old youth batteries forever."

He didn't know if he was more annoyed or flattered that she cared enough to try to browbeat him into the nutritional lifestyle. No one but his grandmother had ever tried to do that before. He supposed he ought to appreciate Abby's interest in his welfare. If only he believed it was for real.

"Okay, listen. I'm giving you this as a gift." He waited until she was looking into his eyes again, then he gave her a grimace of satisfaction. "I stopped at the Hungry Corner and had a three-egg omelet this morning. Satisfied?"

Her eyes actually did light up. "I'm so glad!"

His wide mouth tilted in a half smile. "Yes, it appears I may just live another day."

Abby grinned. "And for that, you can thank a chicken, mister."

Phoebe laughed out loud, and then Daniel

couldn't help but join her, with Abby pealing in a moment later.

"You two," Phoebe said as she regained her composure. "The way you do go on. One minute I'm afraid I'm going to have to call in a referee to keep you from coming to blows, and the next you're chortling together like old friends. Make up your minds! Friend or foe?"

"Both," Daniel said acidly. "We've got issues."

"Do we?" Abby said, looking surprised.

"Yes," Daniel said firmly. "Only we can't talk about them."

She blinked at him, looking blank. "Why not?"

He shrugged. He couldn't tell her the whole truth. Still, he had to say something. "I don't know. It seems to be a rule or something." He glared at her, leaving no doubt that he didn't want to go on with this line of conversation.

"Oh."

That obviously left her puzzled. What the hell. She was hardly the Lone Ranger when it came to puzzlement. He was puzzled by everything life was throwing at him right now.

A nurse came in to check Phoebe's temperature and blood pressure, and Daniel and Abby rose and stepped outside to give her some privacy. They stood side by side, leaning against the hallway wall.

"Listen," he said, giving Abby his hard-as-nails stare, developed over the years to make perps come clean. "Tell me about the atomizer."

"The atomizer?" Her puzzlement was deepening in a regrettably believable way. "What atomizer?"

"The atomizer used by the clinic."

Her brow furled, making her look cuter than a beagle puppy, and she thought hard, then shook her head. "I don't know anything about any atomizer," she told him.

He believed her. He had experience with liars and what they were was exactly what she wasn't.

"You've got the new product list printed, don't you?" he asked.

She nodded. "I can look again, but I'm pretty sure I've got a handle on the whole line now, and I haven't seen anything about any atomizer."

He caught a hint of her scent, and glancing down, his gaze fell on her beautiful mouth and suddenly all thoughts of atomizers faded from his mind. Here she was, pretty in pink and close enough to grab, and he wanted her so badly he could hardly see straight. Who cared about the clinic? Who cared if her attraction to him wasn't real? He wanted her anyway, wanted her so much he actually glanced at the next-door room, wondering if it was empty, before he caught himself and let out an unpleasant expletive.

"Hey," Abby said, looking disapproving, "watch out. There are children around."

For some reason that made him laugh, and she joined in, although it was obvious she had no idea what was so funny. Her gaze met his and something passed between them. Daniel steeled himself. This was no good.

The nurse left and they went back into the room.

"I've got to get going," Daniel said to his grandmother.

"Me, too," Abby said.

Phoebe grabbed her hand, not letting her go. "Wait a minute. I have something I want to say. Daniel, did you get that envelope out of the top drawer of the desk in the den that I asked you to bring me?"

Daniel reached into his pocket and pulled out

a small envelope. "Sure did. Looks like tickets to the Opera Center." He handed it to her. "What are you planning to see there?"

Phoebe took the envelope and peeked inside, smiling. "*Madame Butterfly*. The tickets are for next Monday."

Daniel grimaced. "You won't be out of here yet, I'm afraid. At least, from what the doctor told me this morning."

She nodded happily. "I know that. I'm going to have to miss it. But you two will go in my place. Won't you?"

"What?" they both cried in unison.

"It's the perfect solution." She beamed at them. "I can't stand to think of my two seats sitting empty during the performance. But if you two go…"

"I can't go," Daniel said quickly.

Phoebe's smile dimmed. "Why not?" Her challenge was sharp.

"I'm going to be busy."

"Doing what?"

"Gram!"

She grabbed his hand and squeezed very hard, reaching out and taking Abby's hand again as well.

"Please go," she said, her face anxious. "As a favor to me."

His jaw tightened. She looked so small and vulnerable. He glanced sideways at Abby. She was staring at him, her eyes wide.

"Do you want to go?" he asked gruffly.

"I've never been to the opera," she said.

He gave her a half smile of surrender. "Then I guess it's time you went," he said.

Phoebe sighed happily and fell back against her pillows. "You don't have to stay for the whole thing," she said, suddenly visibly weakening. "If you hate it, you can leave at intermission."

Daniel leaned down and kissed her forehead. "We won't hate it," he promised her, taking the tickets. "Thanks, Gram. Now you get some rest."

Abby thanked her, too, and they started to leave the room together.

"Daniel!"

He turned back to see what she wanted. She motioned for him to lean close and spoke softly.

"You come back when you can. Alone." She grinned at him mischievously. "I've got something for you."

"What?"

"On the case, I mean." She winked at him significantly.

"Oh, that."

"Yes, that. Come back this afternoon and I'll tell you everything."

He smiled at her indulgently. "Okay, Gram. You take a nap in the meantime."

"I'll try to," she said, her voice trailing after him as he made his way out. "But they'll be bringing in a tray and forcing me to eat something soon."

He waved from the doorway, then found, to his surprise, that Abby was waiting for him in the hall.

"Is anything wrong?" she asked, looking a bit anxious.

"No. She just wanted to tell me something." He studied her face, touched by her concern. "Thanks for being so nice to her," he added gruffly.

Her smile lit the area. "Oh, that's no trouble at all. She's a peach."

"She is that," he agreed. It was nice to meet a woman who was concerned about other people as much as she was about anything. Nice—and unusual. Still, he had certain concerns himself.

"But listen," he added, frowning slightly, "don't encourage her about the cruise thing, okay? It's impossible. She can't go. I don't want to see her getting her hopes up."

"Really?" Abby looked as though it mattered to her that Phoebe would be disappointed. "That's a shame. She is so looking forward to it."

He shook his head. He wasn't going into it any further, but he wanted her to know there was no use pursuing it. "Can't be done," he said shortly.

Then he hesitated. The next step would be to ask if she was busy for lunch, wouldn't it? After all, if they were going to the opera together, what harm would an hour for lunch do? It was on the tip of his tongue, when she gave him a brief smile and turned to go.

"Well, I have to get back to work," she said.

He hesitated, then turned, too, and walked beside her toward the elevator. The moment had passed and he was glad it had. Hanging with this angel in pink could get to be dangerous. Best to avoid it. But that didn't mean he wasn't a bit resentful that she'd stayed around, tempting him, and then snatched temptation out of his reach just when he'd begun to weaken.

"Got a meeting with the great Dr. Richie?" he said, unable to keep the sarcasm out of his voice.

"No," she answered as they stepped onto the elevator. "Not at all." She turned to face him, looking up into his eyes. "Why would that be so bad, anyway?"

"No reason." He shrugged, regretting it already. It wouldn't do to make her think he cared. "Forget I said that."

"Okay." The elevator doors opened and she stepped off. "See you next Monday?"

"Sure. I'll come by and get you about six-thirty. Okay?"

She dazzled him with a smile even brighter than the ones he'd already survived. "Okay."

And she was off down the corridor, heading for the clinic. But he didn't move. He'd just looked at the sun and it was a few moments before he could shake off the blindness.

Six

Abby was walking on air and she wasn't really sure why. Daniel was acting strangely, being obstinate, trying to hold back from allowing anything to grow between them. She wasn't sure why that was, either. But she wasn't going to let it rain on her parade.

"I'm going to the opera," she reminded herself, laughing softly to think of Daniel listening to tenors and sopranos. Heavy metal would have seemed more his taste. Regardless, it was going to be an adventure. And she hoped there would be more kissing involved. At the very least.

Walking quickly toward her office, she noticed someone in the courtyard. Ordinarily that wouldn't have occasioned a second glance, but there was something about the woman that seemed odd. She almost seemed to be skulking.

It wasn't until Abby stepped out into the open-air atrium that she realized she recognized the woman as someone she'd seen before. She was short and attractively compact, and her blond hair shone in the sunlight. Large dark glasses hid her eyes.

"Hello, there," Abby called to her. "Can I help you?"

The woman jumped, startled, and for a second or two looked definitely guilty. "Oh, uh…"

Abby walked forward, hand outstretched. "My name is Abby Edwards and I'm the public relations representative for the clinic."

The woman tried to smile but made sad work of it. Still, she did take Abby's offer of a handshake. "Carrie Martin," she said.

"I've seen you at some of the seminars."

"Have you?"

"Yes. But you've never come forward and registered for any of the classes." Abby smiled at her. "Tell me…what's your hesitation?"

Carrie seemed not to hear her at first. She kept turning to gaze into the conference room that could be seen through a bank of large windows. She didn't look so much confused as distracted. Glancing at Abby, she said, "I—I guess I'm just not ready…"

Abby frowned, not sure how to approach this. Still, she had to try to do something. The woman obviously was unhappy in some way. Surely the clinic could give her assistance. That was what they were here for—or at any rate, that was what she was writing up in the brochures.

"Let me see if I can help you." Abby took her hand again, looking into her face with a genuine compassion. "I can call one of our counselors to come over right now and—"

"No!" Carrie pulled her hand away quickly. "No, no. I don't want to do that. I don't need counseling."

Abby frowned thoughtfully. "Who would you like to see, then?"

Carrie looked away and half laughed. "Your Dr. Richie, actually."

"Tell you what." Abby brightened. "I'm going over to his office right now. Would you like to come along and—"

"Dr. Richie?" Carrie looked surprised. "I could talk to him right now?"

"Sure. It's not the way we usually operate, but I think I could get him to speak to you for just a moment or two. Would you like to meet him?"

"Yes," she said, sounding a bit breathless. "Of course."

"Then let's go." Abby turned toward the door that led to his office.

But Carrie drew back. "No! Oh, no. I'm not ready for that."

Abby smiled encouragingly. "He doesn't bite, believe me. He's a very nice man."

"Is he?" She seemed to be really asking the question. Lifting her dark glasses, she stared at Abby for a long moment as though trying to figure her out. "How well do you know him?"

"Well, I've only been working here for a few weeks, but…"

The glasses dropped in place again and she shrugged. "That explains it." Turning, she headed for the exit. "Thanks, but no thanks," she called back. "Another time maybe."

Abby watched her go, shaking her head.

Maybe she just didn't have the knack. She would have to talk to Dr. Richie about it.

Carrie Martin seemed troubled, but she was quite an attractive woman who carried herself as though she were aware, educated and bright. So why did she seem to be in another world? Hard to say.

Abby turned back toward her office, planning to pick up a few papers and go on over to see Dr. Richie. As she turned, she caught sight of herself in the glass and she had to stop and stare in astonishment. Her skirt was downright loose! That formula of the doctor's really did work.

She shrugged, made a face at herself in the glass. "He's a genius," she reminded herself. "And I'm glad I work for him."

And she didn't care what Daniel had to say about the matter. Though she had to admit, his cynicism was beginning to bother her a bit. He saw the clinic and the doctor from a very different perspective. He didn't understand that working with this institution was a life saver for her. Dr. Richie was giving her a chance. She would be forever grateful to him for that alone. Daniel just didn't understand.

Well then, it was her duty to bring him to the

truth of the situation. Good thing she was going to have a chance when they went to the opera.

The opera! What did one wear to the opera? Something fabulous, of course. She did a quick mental inventory of her closet and knew there wasn't one thing fabulous in it. No problem. The mall was only blocks away. She could easily take an hour off and do some quick shopping.

Something long and slinky, she thought, half dreaming. Something with lots of glittery stuff on it. Something completely different from anything she'd ever owned before. After all, she was skinny enough now. And after only a few days. Of course, she'd only had a few pounds to lose. She might as well quit using it. She'd lost enough weight and she hated letting anything artificial affect her in any way. So the experiment was over, as far as she was concerned.

"Test successful," she jotted down on her calendar, making a mental note to check just how much she had lost on her scale that evening.

And now to drop in to see Dr. Richie—and then, to the mall!

Daniel was back in his grandmother's room later in the afternoon. He'd had another talk with her doctor and he was worried. There seemed to be evidence of blood clotting in the veins of her legs, something that had put her in the hospital earlier in the summer.

"We've got her on a strong anticoagulant," the doctor told him. "But she's got to be carefully watched. Blood thinners can be dangerous. I'm afraid we were right and it will be a few more days before we dare let her go home."

The news hit him harder than he expected. His grandmother had always been so healthy until the last few months. The fall had been tough to take, but it was a normal occurrence. Blood clots were something else again, something he didn't know how to detect or deal with. In his line of work he knew very well that the unknown was usually much scarier than the known. And yet he was scared. He couldn't help it. She was the only parent figure he'd known for years and he didn't want to lose her. Not yet.

Looking at her gray hair against the light-blue pillow, he felt a wave of affection for her and his eyes stung a little. It took a moment for him to realize the sting just might be a threat of tears. He fought that back quickly. No way was he going to start bawling.

"Hey," he said to her, trying to be cheerful. "What's up?"

"Oh." She opened her eyes and beamed at him. "I'm so glad you're here. I've got things to tell you." She looked behind him. "Check the door. Is there anyone in the hall?"

She made him smile; she was having so much fun with this. So, despite the fact that he didn't expect to get much out of it, he did as she ordered, checking to make sure no one could overhear them. Then he came back and sat in the chair beside her bed.

"Okay. Here goes." She settled back against the pillows, getting comfortable. "Arline—that's the little redheaded nurse—"

"Yes, I know Arline."

"She stopped in and I got her talking about the clinic."

"Did you?"

"Yes. I asked her what it used to be like before Dr. Richie came and she really opened up. I got a whole load of gossip."

Gossip. Relationships. He said, she said.

He groaned silently. This could go on for hours. He only hoped there would be some real information to be gleaned from it. You never did know.

"I'll skip most of the feuds and the indiscretions and the baby found in the clothes hamper. Oh, and the alligator races. Save all that stuff for another day. I want to give you the relevant info in a nutshell."

"Alligator races?"

She patted his hand. "It's a long story. Anyway, the crux of the matter is that Dr. Richie was hired against the wishes of some of the most senior members of the hospital board."

Daniel raised an eyebrow. "You don't say."

"It seems that a certain Faye Lassen had been groomed for the role."

Daniel nodded. "I know Faye. She helps out at the seminars."

"Well, she was working her little fingers to the bone with high expectations, and when Dr. Richie came barreling into town, sweeping all before him with a media frenzy, poor Faye was left gaping like a fish out of water. The position she expected, the one she'd been laying all the groundwork for, went to the new guy with the TV-friendly smile."

"Poor Faye indeed."

"Yes." Phoebe looked thoughtful. "I think I knew her mother. Nice woman. Large teeth. Tended to snort when she laughed, but otherwise—"

"Gram, you're straying from the subject."

"So I am. Well, it seems this Faye does have a few partisans, but on the whole, everyone has become so infatuated with the glittering celebrity of Dr. Richie, there seems to be little hope that Faye will ever be recognized for all her hard work and good deeds. Arline thinks resentment is smoldering." Phoebe gave him a wise look. "Motivation for mischief?" she suggested significantly.

Daniel looked innocent. "What mischief?"

"Well, I don't know," she said indignantly. "But I'm sure if you're on a case involving the clinic, then there's mischief afoot. As night follows day."

Daniel laughed. "If everyone had a grandmother as crafty as you, the world would be in total chaos," he said.

"You're avoiding my question."

"Sorry, Gram. I'm going to have to plead the fifth on that one."

"Oh!" She wrinkled her nose in frustration. "You can trust me."

"You have no need to know."

"Then tell me about you and Abby. What's going on?"

His frown was meant to stop this line of questioning in its tracks. "There is nothing going on between me and Abby."

Her skeptical look gave that statement just what it deserved.

"Does she know you're a cop?"

He hesitated, wincing a little. "No. At least, I haven't told her."

Phoebe nodded. "It's time you told her."

He knew that. But right now it wouldn't be helpful.

"I'll tell her just as soon as I can. Once I have this investigation under control."

"That'll be too late," Phoebe told him wisely. "Tell her now. And to heck with your investigation."

Easy for you to say, he thought to himself as he made his way down the hall. To heck with his investigation, huh? Might as well say to heck with his job, his life, his self-worth. He couldn't join his grandmother. A man didn't throw away everything that mattered to him just because a woman under some bogus love spell was making eyes at him.

He turned a corner and there she was, coming toward him at a brisk pace, walking side by side with Dr. Richie. She was nodding at something the doctor was saying but her eyes met Daniel's and she brightened visibly.

Dr. Richie didn't spare him a glance. He passed without acknowledging Daniel's existence, but Abby gave him a wink and a secret smile that somehow managed to convey the sense of having a private joke that was understood by just the two of them and no one else.

Suddenly she wheeled and turned back, hurrying up to Daniel and whispering near his ear.

"I found out about the atomizers."

"You did?"

"Yes, I did. I'll call you later and I'll tell you all about it."

A quick, mischievous grin and she was off, catching up with the doctor before he even noticed she'd been gone.

Daniel turned and watched as they disappeared

around the corner and found himself grinning like a loon for no reason whatsoever. Quickly he doused it. What was wrong with him anyway? She managed to get to him somehow, every time.

He was going to go home and have a beer and watch some baseball and forget all about Abby Edwards and her pretty face and nicely rounded body. If he could.

Rain. Steady, depressing rain.

So what else was new? Rain in Portland? What a surprise.

Daniel turned up the collar on his windbreaker and walked quickly from the parking lot to the hospital. The puddle by the entryway was as large as a lake. Something was leaking somewhere. He edged his way around the water, centered and wiped his feet on the length of mat that had been laid down for that purpose, grumbling all the way. Looking up, he saw Wilbur Mason coming out of Ella Crown's shop.

"Here," Ella said, following him out and slapping a box of candy in his hands. "I don't want your presents. I don't want your poems. I don't want your love letters. I don't want you hanging around like a lovesick goat. Just stay away from me! Do you understand?"

Daniel looked at Wilbur, expecting to see a hangdog to be pitied. Instead, the man seemed to be responding strangely to Ella's rejection.

"Ella, Ella, Ella," he was saying, a goofy smirk on his face. "You're so cute when you're mad." His face changed. "I know what'll get ya," he said, looking as though he'd just discovered the secret of life. "A serenade." He snapped his fingers, seeming to be talking to himself. "A Spanish song. A rose between my teeth. That'll do it."

Turning on his heel, he almost ran into Daniel.

"'Scuse me, I've got to go learn how to play the guitar," he told him pleasantly, moving along like a much younger man.

Ella watched him go, her hands on her hips. She looked as though she was about to emit steam from her ears.

"Did you hear that old coot?" she demanded of Daniel. "All these years I thought he was a decent sort. He's a Portland archivist, you know. He once interviewed me about my family. Pioneers, city founders and all that. I kind of liked him. Didn't know he was crazy." She shook her head and looked earnestly into Daniel's eyes. "There's something weird going on in this place. Watch yourself. Don't let them get you, too."

She started to go back into her shop but Daniel stopped her.

"What do you mean?" he asked her. "Who do you think is out to 'get' us?"

She shook her head. "You got me. It's driving me nuts. I may have to go to one of that cutie-pie Dr. Richie's seminars to learn how to relieve my stress." She made a sound that indicated what she thought of that nonsense. "I'm just warning you, because you seem to be one of the few who are still sane." She gave him a pointed look. "You remember that movie, with the pods changing people into aliens?"

"Oh, yes. One of my favorites."

She nodded. "Don't go into any basements, okay?"

"Okay." He grinned at her, but she didn't smile back. Snorting, she went inside her flower shop.

Daniel's cell phone rang at the same time. He flipped it open and barked, "O'Callahan here."

"Hey, Danny boy. I got the results of those tests you wanted run."

Daniel straightened. "Great. That was fast work. Let's have it."

"Okay. The lab tech gave me all kinds of gobbledy-gook but the bottom line is, you ain't got squat."

"Nothing?"

"Nope. Zero, zip, nada."

Daniel shook his head in disgust. "Even on the nutrition bar?"

"It's a nutrition bar. What can I say?"

"With nothing strange in it?" He was begging for a tiny piece of something, anything, just to help him know which way to turn.

But Jimmy couldn't bail him out.

"Nope," he said. "What were you expecting anyway?"

"You wouldn't believe me if I told you."

"Try me."

Daniel hesitated, then grinned. "An aphrodisiac. How do you like that?"

Jimmy brightened. "I don't know. I haven't tried it yet."

"And you never will. I'm trying to protect people from it, not promote it."

"What a killjoy," Jimmy muttered kiddingly.

Then he sobered. "Hey, I'll send over the complete analysis. There are sheets and sheets of it."

"Okay." Daniel sighed heavily. He'd hoped to wrap this up quickly but obviously it was going to take more research and investigation than he'd thought. "Thanks, Jimmy. I owe you one."

"You don't owe me nothin'." Jimmy's voice changed a bit. He cleared his throat. It was a pretty good bet he was going to launch into a topic that was not completely comfortable for him. "So what's the latest you hear from the inquiry?"

"Nothing yet."

"Ah, come on, they're gonna clear you. You know that."

"No, I don't know that."

There was certainly a possibility that the inquiry might give someone the excuse they needed to have him kicked off the force. Some powerful political movers and shakers had it in for him now. He knew very well that a fair hearing would exonerate him completely. But whether or not the hearing would be fair—that was the question.

Still, he didn't like to waste mental energy worrying about something he couldn't do anything about. If it happened, it happened. There was no use losing sleep over it.

Back to the dopey love epidemic. Keeping his mind busy on that kept it off the inquiry.

He rang off from Jimmy and dropped in to see his grandmother. She was feeling better and looking very perky. They exchanged a few jokes and anecdotes until a slender dark-haired woman appeared in the doorway.

"Ah, here's the physical therapist," his grandmother said with a grimace. "Time for my daily torture."

Daniel nodded at the pleasant-looking young woman. "Gram, do you want me to stay and—"

"Oh, get on with you. You must have something better to do. And I don't really want you to see me in my hour of distress."

He gave her a kiss and left, promising to be back in the afternoon. As he turned out of the room, he almost collided with Abby coming toward him from the elevators. She smiled.

"Going my way?" she asked.

Seven

Daniel took a quick breath to steady himself. The last thing he wanted was to let Abby know how strongly she affected the way his body worked.

"That depends. Which way are you going?"

She motioned with her head. "I'm heading to the cafeteria to get something to eat."

He raised an eyebrow. "Something to eat. Hmm."

"I know, I know. You think it's a little early for lunch."

"And a little late for breakfast."

"So let's call it brunch."

He snapped his fingers. "The woman has the gift."

She looked pleased, tucking her hand into the crook of his arm as though he'd already agreed to go with her. "Yes. I'm just glad you're smart enough to recognize it." She sighed. "Actually, I'm ravenous. I spent the morning organizing a session of exercise therapy."

"Ah. The exercises." He raised an eyebrow. "I hope you weren't doing the old Giaza with someone other than me. That's our special exercise, you know."

She laughed and seemed to pull him closer.

He supposed he'd been recruited for brunch, but he couldn't conjure up any reason not to join her. And he wasn't sure he would have used any of those reasons if he could have thought of them. Her hand felt too good on his arm. In fact, just being with her was making him happy.

Happy wasn't one of his usual emotions. He was a cop, for God's sake. *Happy* had nothing to do with the life he'd led and expected to lead in the future. Getting the job done. Satisfaction in his role in protecting society against the bad guys. Making the world safe for little kids to grow up without pain and horror. That was what he was all about. Not being *happy*.

Forget happy and get back to work.

"You were going to tell me about the atomizer."

He'd just about decided the atomizer was his last hope in finding the culprit, but somehow the concept wasn't striking much excitement in his mind. If it were the guilty element, it would seem more people would have heard of it. But he was ready to take any information she was ready to give, just to add it in to the brew.

"Ah, the atomizer. Yes." She smiled at him sideways. "You know that Dr. Richie had a long history of therapeutic counseling and wellness instruction before he came here. Well, the atomizer was something he was working with a few years ago when he came through Portland doing his workshops. From what he says, it was more related to aromatherapy than weight control."

She frowned, thinking of something. "It may have been the first permutation of the NoWait oil, though, come to think of it. Anyway, he abandoned it a long time ago. Anyone who has an atomizer must have been at those original workshops."

Daniel nodded. He'd had a feeling it was something like that. Still, it didn't help break through this dead end he seemed to be facing.

"Maybe it's time I got an interview with the great man himself," he murmured, almost as much to himself as to her.

"He's so busy," she said evasively. "But I'll see what I can do."

"I'd appreciate it."

"He doesn't like giving interviews. He says that's what he hired me for."

"Doesn't like interviews?" He looked at her, incredulous. "What are you talking about? He's on television all the time."

"Yes, but that's different. That has nothing to do with him personally."

That fit, all right. Sounded like a totally guilty man to him.

They reached the cafeteria and he held the door for her.

"Mmm, you smell good," she murmured, skimming close to him as she passed.

"Me?" He was taken aback. "I'm not wearing any cologne or anything."

"I know." She smiled up at him, so close he was tempted to wrap his arms around her. "Clean male. The best scent there is."

She turned to enter the cafeteria line, but he had to wait a moment, pretending to read the notices on the wall, before he could follow her. He'd never before known a woman who could turn him on in seconds. Maybe he ought to see if Dr. Richie had an antidote.

Abby had already started a tray and a cute little dark-haired nurse had come between them, so he picked up a tray for himself. The nurse turned and looked into his face and gave a sigh that could have been heard in the parking lot.

"Oh! Green eyes. I would die for a man with green eyes."

Great. Another victim of Dr. Richie's love potion.

"Not here, please," Daniel told her curtly. "You'll clutter up the food line."

She laughed and leaned toward him like a tree in a strong wind. He could see Abby turning and noticing what was going on, so he flashed the little nurse a look. But she didn't notice.

"You're cute," she said. "Can I sit with you?"

"I'm sorry. I'm afraid I already have a companion." He nodded his head in Abby's direction, and she smiled, giving the nurse a friendly little wave.

The nurse's face fell. "Okay, then," she said sadly. "Well, in case she flakes out on you, I'll be at that table in the corner. I'll be watching." She smiled at him sunnily. "Every move."

"Better not," he advised sardonically. "You'll make me nervous. I'm liable to drop my fork or something."

She giggled. "If you drop a fork, I'll swoop down and pick it up for you, Mr. Green Eyes."

"Don't bother," he told her. "I think we'll be able to handle the silverware."

He took advantage of her momentary lack of attention to push past her and join Abby in time to pay for both of them. Abby gave him a look full of amusement but she didn't say anything until they'd chosen their table and sat down, setting out on the table between them Abby's bagel and cream cheese and Daniel's toast and smoked salmon, along with their tea and lingonberry jam.

"My gosh, I didn't realize you were such a babe magnet," Abby said, laughing.

He shook his head, feeling exasperated. "It's been like this all week."

She nodded wisely, taking a bite from her bagel. "I'll bet it's been like this all your life."

He decided to level with her. Why not? Maybe it was time they got some of their cards out on the table.

"You'd lose that bet. It's just been this last week or so. And do you know why?"

Her eyes widened, chewing suspended. "No. Tell me."

He looked around the room. "If you go and ask these people—the lovesick ones I mean—every one of them will have some connection to the clinic."

She made a skeptical face. "How can you know that?"

He shrugged. "Try it." He took a bite of his toast, generously loaded with pink salmon.

She stared at him, and, for just a moment, she looked uncertain. Then she shook her head. "Let me get this straight. You think some sort of love virus is going around and the clinic is the carrier?"

His gaze was steady and sure. "You got it."

"That's crazy."

He shrugged again. "Call me a nut case."

"I might just have to. I think you're reading things into the fact that people who've been to the clinic are happier people and more likely to be friendly. That's all."

"It's more than that. You haven't noticed that it's like a looney bin around here?"

"No."

"Everyone is falling madly in love with the first person they meet up with in the morning."

"You're exaggerating." She made a face at him. "Just because Dr. Richie's lectures and other things at the clinic are giving people a feeling of well-being and giving them the confidence to express feelings they may have hidden for years—"

"It's much more than that and you know it."

"No, I don't."

His attention was diverted as he noticed a stocky, balding man heading toward their table with an intensity Daniel was beginning to recognize as common around the hospital. The man's gaze was fixed lovingly on Abby.

"Look out," Daniel warned in a low voice. "Male suspect at three o'clock and closing fast."

"What are you talking about?" She glanced around and saw the man, then smiled briefly, putting down her teacup. "Hello, Dr. Porter."

"Abby. Ah, Abby." The smitten man took her hand between both of his and brought it to his lips. Abby looked startled.

"Well, I'm...glad to see you, too."

Dr. Porter gazed at her with all the devotion of a lovesick cocker spaniel. "Abby, my dear, you don't know how you've changed my life."

"I have?" Abby looked as though she regretted whatever she'd done to bring on this salute.

"Yes. Since you got me involved at the clinic, I'm a changed person." Dr. Porter glanced sideways at Daniel, seeming to notice him for the first time, but apparently the doctor decided to ignore him for the moment. "And, Abby, it's all because of you."

"Well, I'm so glad."

"Look. I've already lost ten pounds."

"Good for you."

He glanced at Daniel again, frowning slightly, and seemed to decide he couldn't ignore him any longer. "Uh, Abby, who is this man?" He motioned toward Daniel. "A mere colleague I hope? Not a significant other?"

Abby looked at Daniel. "Well, uh, this is…"

"Her fiancé," Daniel said firmly, rising and sticking out his hand. "Daniel O'Callahan. Nice to meet you, Doctor."

Abby's jaw had dropped, so Daniel felt he'd better keep the doctor's attention aimed his way for a moment or two more. "Yup, wedding in June and all that."

"June?" Dr. Porter looked suspicious. "It's August right now."

"So it is. Well, we both believe in long engagements, don't we, Abby darling?"

Abby had regained control of her jaw, but her eyes were big as saucers. "What?" she said breathlessly.

"Sweetie-pie? Better half? Demon lover?" He grinned at her. "You tell me which you like best."

Dr. Porter drew back as though he'd been stung. From the look on his face, one would have to conclude he didn't approve.

"Such a shame," he muttered, nodding to the two of them before shuffling off toward a table full of nurses.

"You see what I mean?" Daniel told Abby. "He's been to the clinic and caught the bug."

She frowned. "Then why haven't you caught it? And why haven't I caught it?"

He winced at the last question, but answered the first. "I haven't used any of the clinic products."

Abby was staring at him and he had the distinct impression she was finally understanding what this was all about, even if she didn't recognize the fact that she was tied up in it all. What was he going to say to her? How could he gently get her to look at her own changes, analyze them, see where they came from? And once he did that, was she going to hate him? He knew how she was going to feel once she realized he was a cop, investigating her precious clinic—and her precious Dr. Richie. And he wasn't looking forward to it.

Abby pushed her food away, but before she could launch into whatever lecture she was preparing in her head, Wilbur Mason came in and approached their table. The man had lost his usual sunny composure. He looked as though he'd just lost his best friend as well.

"What is it, Wilbur?" Daniel asked. "You'd better sit down."

He did so, heavily, and leaned both elbows on the tabletop. "Ella won't speak to me," he said, tragedy etching lines in his face. "She won't even let me in her shop."

Daniel glanced at Abby. Ella often acted annoyed with Wilbur, but Daniel had had the impression she secretly liked the attention.

"Did you try the serenade idea yet?" he asked.

"No." Wilbur brightened a bit. "But I did find a great guitar at the pawn shop."

"Good. Start practicing and get yourself a rose bush."

Wilbur sat a little taller. "That's exactly what I'm planning to do." Color began returning to his cheeks. "It may take me a while." He frowned doubtfully and looked at Daniel. "Do you think I've got enough time?"

"Of course you do. You've got forever, in your own terms." Daniel had no idea what that meant, but it sounded good, and all he wanted to do was comfort the man and buck him up a bit.

"Very true, young man." Wilbur was looking like his old self again. "That's very wise." He smiled. "Ah, Ella, Ella. She's so lovely."

Daniel's left eyebrow rose all of its own accord. "Yes," he murmured, "especially with the blue eye shadow."

Abby kicked him under the table, but Wilbur hadn't noticed anything amiss. He was full of confidence again. "I'd better get going," he said, rising from his chair. "I've got a guitar lesson in half an hour. Wish me luck!"

And he was off. Daniel turned to Abby with a questioning look. "Are you beginning to get the picture here?"

She squirmed uncomfortably. "Daniel, I think you should have a bit more compassion for these people. Can't you be a little more sensitive to their pain?"

He leaned toward her. "And I think you need to be a little less naive. Something fishy is going on at that clinic."

She stared back at him, and he could see that she knew he was right.

"So," she said softly, "what do you plan to do about it?"

Carrie Martin stared out at the pouring rain. Sheltered by the spacious kiosk situated outside the hospital, she was waiting for the bus that would take her to her job as hostess at La Grenouille Dorée, one of Portland's fanciest restaurants. And her feet hurt.

"You'll get used to it," she kept telling herself. She had formerly taught math at a private school in San Francisco. She'd had to stand a lot at that, too, but somehow it just wasn't as rough on her feet as hostessing was.

"Oh, well, you won't have to do this much longer."

That was the second thing she kept telling herself. She'd come to Portland with one goal in mind—confronting her ex-husband, Richard Strokudnowski, known to the world as Dr. Richie Strong. She'd been here for weeks and she hadn't summoned up enough nerve to do it yet. In fact, she was spending far too much time in a state of ambivalence. Did she really need to do this? Would it change anything?

Yes. Some things had to be said. And the people who were being taken in by the false image he was projecting to the world needed to be given a wake-up call. Somehow she was going to have to gather together the nerve to do it. Somehow.

Hearing the unmistakable sound of someone running through the rain, she turned in time to see Daniel O'Callahan arrive at the kiosk, stopping in for a moment of shelter from the downpour.

"Welcome to my little island," she told him humorously as he shook off the water and blinked at her.

"Oh, hello," he said. "I'm was on the way to my car, but the sky opened up. It's really coming down. I thought I'd give it a minute before I go on."

"Good idea."

He looked at her with interest. "Carrie Martin, isn't it?"

"Yes. We met the other night at the clinic seminar."

"I remember. The mysterious lady who wanted a gallon of ice cream all to herself."

"In the spirit of rebellion," she said, nodding. "And what were you doing there? You hardly look like someone in need of weight control."

He hesitated, then told her, "Actually I was just doing a little investigating."

"Ah-ha. Cop, private eye or media?"

"Uh, nothing official."

"I see. A freelancer."

"Well, not exactly."

She laughed. "Don't worry. I won't pry into your agenda. I have my own to take care of. And that's quite enough to complicate my life thoroughly."

He smiled his appreciation, remembering that he had thought at the time that this lady might hold information he would need to get to the bottom of things. She seemed more open to talking today, more approachable. So why not see what could be gleaned?

"Okay, Carrie Martin," he said, smiling at her. "Both our agendas aside, what do you know about Dr. Richie that I should know?"

A veil seemed to drop over her eyes. "What makes you think I know anything special about him?" she asked after a long pause.

"A hunch. One of those hair-prickling-on-the-back-of-my-neck sort of hunches."

She looked at him closely, and finally, she laughed. "Ooh, that sounds serious."

He gazed at her somberly. "It is."

She looked away, then looked into his eyes again. "Tell you what. If I have anything to say, you'll be among the first to hear it."

He hesitated for a moment, then nodded. "It's a deal."

She shook her head. "So impatient," she murmured. "You've already got enough on your plate from the looks of it. I saw you an hour or so ago in the cafeteria with Abby Edwards."

"Yeah, we were…having brunch."

To her amusement, he seemed almost embarrassed and she could have sworn his face got a bit redder. Evidence of love in bloom if she ever saw it. It warmed her and made her envious at the same time. She'd had those feelings once. They hadn't lasted though, had they?

"Listen, can I give you a ride?" Daniel asked. "I could get my car and drive over here and—"

"No, no. Thanks, but I'm waiting for my bus. It takes me right to where I'm going. I'm fine."

"Okay." He looked out, grimacing. "I guess it's lightened up a little. I'm going to make a run for it. See you later."

"Good-bye."

She watched him dash through the rain and heard someone else coming up from the direction of the hospital. Turning, she almost gasped aloud. It was the famous clinic doctor himself, holding a newspaper over his head against the drops.

"Wow," he said, smiling at her as he shook off the wetness like a large friendly dog. "I didn't realize it had gone from drizzle to full-scale pouring rain."

She must have muttered something in reply, but she couldn't have said what it was. This was the first time she'd been so close to the man in almost twenty years. She wasn't ready for this!

What would she do if he recognized her? Of course, she'd changed. The years had done their work, but she'd also lost fifty pounds, dyed her hair blond and was wearing contacts that gave her the appearance of having blue eyes. Still, there was the voice. That was the hardest thing to disguise, but she would do her best by remembering to speak in a low tone.

He was still talking, going on and on about rain and the weather in Portland. She was regaining control as he spoke, catching her breath and managing a pleasant smile, despite the fact that her heart was beating so hard, it seemed to blot out thought. He was being friendly, much warmer and more personable than he seemed when he was talking to the groups she'd attended lately.

Almost like the old Richard, she thought.

But it would be better not to have thoughts like that.

"I'm Dr. Richie," he was saying, holding out his hand.

She froze for a moment, unable to make herself touch him. But it had to be done. With a jerky motion, she reached out and let him take her hand in his.

"C-C-Carrie Martin," she managed to stutter out, then drew her hand back.

"You intrigue me, Carrie," he said, frowning slightly. "Something about you reminds me of someone I used to know long ago."

Oh, no! "Really?" *Hold on, don't lose it now.* "The love of your life, no doubt." *Oh, my God! Did I really say that? What's wrong with me?* She looked anxiously into his face, but he seemed amused.

"Ah, but life is full of many loves," he said. "Don't you agree?"

She blinked. "No, not really." Now she was getting annoyed with him. Anxiety fell away as anger took over.

"No?"

She stared at his reaction. You'd think the man

had never had a statement challenged before. He looked downright shocked that she would take an opposing view.

"No," she said firmly. "I think real love requires a few things deeper than flirtation. Like honesty. Compassion. Fidelity."

He looked a bit bored. "The old-fashioned virtues. They're all well and good for the run-of-the-mill population." His smile managed to convey the idea that sophisticated adults such as the two of them knew better. "But don't you think that there are some people who aspire to something larger and have so much more to give that their spirit can't be confined that way? They need more, they give more, they have more to share with the world."

So this was the claptrap he'd been feeding his ego lately. No wonder it was so flabby. Oh, yes, this was the sort of thing that made her really mad and always had.

"Could it be that others see it differently than you do? Seeing it from another perspective, I mean. In other words, where you see more giving, they might see more taking. Where you see yourself as a sharer, they might see a user."

He shrugged, not particularly affronted by her speculation.

"I doubt that. I think most of my people know where I'm coming from. My people see me for what I am."

"*Your* people?" She was fairly quivering with outrage at that one. "Are you some sort of cult leader, then?"

She thought he'd react with anger, or at least with annoyance, but he laughed and stepped closer to her. The fact that she wasn't falling into line seemed to keep alive the interest he felt in her.

"Listen, I've got a little time before my next appointment," he told her. His smile was patently seductive in a practiced way that must have worked often in his past. "Would you like to go get a cup of coffee?"

She looked at him steadily. By all rights, she should slap his face. The nerve of the man—trying to pick up his own ex-wife.

"No, Dr. Richie," she said loud and clear. "I most definitely would not."

As luck would have it, her bus arrived just at the right time. Giving him a parting glare, she boarded it and made her way to a seat near the back without looking over her shoulder to see his reaction. Her heart was thumping and she was damp with sweat. But she'd told him what she thought. She hadn't weakened on that score.

Closing her eyes, she tried to let the swaying of the bus calm her nerves. Her cell phone rang and she fumbled for it.

"Hello? Oh, Jason." She relaxed. It was her son. "Yes, darling. Don't you worry. I'm taking care of it."

"Mother!" Jason obviously caught the tension in her voice and it worried him. "What are you going to do?"

Her voice hardened and she stared straight ahead. "Take care of business, Jason. Something I should have done years ago."

"No, Mom. What's the point? Leave the man alone. Come home. Get on with your life."

"I can't leave him alone." She turned and muffled her voice so that others on the bus wouldn't hear her conversation. "He's become a monster. I'm the only one who knows just how far he's come from what he used to be. I feel it's my duty to do something about it."

Jason was silent for a long moment, then he asked ominously, "What are you going to do?"

"I'm just working that out myself. But I'm going to do something. And it's going to be soon."

Eight

A huge silver moon hung in the sky. Magic? Could be. Daniel was certainly feeling as though something was pulling his strings. The funny thing was, he sort of liked it.

Every time he let himself look at Abby he felt control slipping further away. He'd managed to stay away from her all weekend, but his date for the opera was hanging over him the whole time. She was gorgeous, dressed in something that fit like a second skin—a very sparkly second skin— with long, glittering earrings that swayed as she walked. She'd added a tiny little white furry thing that was supposed to act as a wrap of sorts and really served to frame her pretty face in a way he found completely irresistible. The ends curved down and followed the line of her breasts, opening at the front to reveal a generous portion of those lovely items. Every time he caught a glimpse of that white, untouched skin, the pit of his stomach dropped as though he'd taken a roller-coaster ride into the night.

He was a sad case, a lost cause—and totally happy about it.

"Now that was quite something," he said, referring to the performance of *Madame Butterfly* they'd just seen. They were walking slowly through the courtyard on their way to the parking lot. They'd loitered inside so long, they practically had the place to themselves by now. Neither one of them seemed to want to hurry the evening toward its conclusion.

"I loved it," Abby declared to the world.

"Did you?"

"You didn't?"

"Hmm." He looked at her sideways. "A lot of the music was pretty good. I don't know. As long as they keep to tenors and mezzos I'm okay, but sopranos tend to blow out my ears and leave me a quivering mass of jelly."

She laughed. "Your quivering was politely subtle. No one noticed." She threw out her arms to the night. "I thought it was all just wonderful."

"Well, it's an event," he responded, shoving his hands into the pockets of his suit coat. "Something everyone should try at least once in his life." He gave her a quick smile, his gaze lingering on those white breasts, then pulling quickly away. "Now you can add it to your list of experiences."

"It's a pretty short list," she said as they paused to gaze into a decorative pond. "Going to the opera will be a major entry on it."

"What do you mean?" He turned and looked at her quizzically.

Instead of answering his question directly, she smiled at him and said, "It's funny to think I've been to the opera but I've never been to a rock concert."

He stared at her, thunderstruck. "You've got to be kidding."

"No. Actually, I haven't done a lot of things that most people my age have done." She looked out at the moon. "I had sort of an unusual childhood."

"Raised in a convent?"

"Not quite. But I was raised to believe hard work and academic success were the only things that mattered. Fun was out. A waste of time. My parents were loving in their own way, but they saw me more as an asset than as a kid. And I realize now that a little more balance in my life would have been better."

He was quiet for a long moment, gazing into the water of the pond. Finally, he turned to her.

"You know what? I'm not going to criticize them."

Her eyebrows rose. "No?"

He shook his head. "No. Whatever they did, they ended up with one pretty great daughter. So who am I to complain?"

She laughed and turned her face up and he kissed her.

It began as a lighthearted gesture. That was all he meant to do, kiss her lightly and move on. But she tasted so sweet he couldn't pull away. Somehow his tongue got involved and her arms came around his neck and his hands were sliding down her sides, cupping her bottom and pulling her close, and there he was, swept with an urgency to have her for his own.

A knot of people started toward them from the concert hall and they broke apart, both panting softly and gazing into each other's eyes. He took her hand in his and started toward the car again.

"Okay," he said firmly. "Next month there's a Journey concert. I've got two tickets. You're coming with me."

She turned her head to look at him as they walked. "Who were you planning to take with you?"

"My grandmother."

Her jaw dropped. "You were not!"

He grinned. "Was, too."

"Oh, you liar!"

"Yes, I really was. She loves Journey."

"But a rock concert?"

His smile dimmed. "She's probably not going to feel like going now that she's had these problems," he admitted. They reached the car and he opened the door to let her in. "So we'll go. Okay?"

She nodded happily. "Okay. But if she feels like going at the last minute…"

"She'll have first dibs," he promised her.

"She's still talking about taking that cruise," Abby noted as they left the parking area and turned onto the street. "She told me today that she's feeling much stronger and thinks she can make it."

His heart fell. He hated to be the one to disappoint her. Glancing at Abby, he remembered that the retirement home he was dealing with was close by and he turned the car toward it, slowing to a stop in front of the main entrance. The entry to the five-story building was lit by a huge chandelier. The extravagant plantings that studded the grounds were lit by tiny lights. Other lights filled the windows and shone along the walkways. It looked like a royal garden, an enchanted retreat from the real world.

And that was exactly what he hoped it would be for his grandmother.

"I wanted you to see this place," Daniel told Abby when she turned to look questioningly at him. "I know everyone's been encouraging her to go on that cruise to Alaska. And I know you've wondered why I'm so dead set against it. Well, here's one of the main reasons she can't go."

He gestured toward the residence. Even from where they were sitting it was obviously a stylish, well-appointed place.

"She's reached the age where she requires some extra care and extra help, things I can't give her the way she needs. I want her to be comfortable. I want her to be happy and safe and among really nice people who will care about her."

Abby looked from him to the residence and back again. "It...it certainly looks like a lovely place."

He heard the doubt in her voice and he knew it wasn't about the quality of the home.

"Look," he said, trying mightily to keep the defensive tone out of his voice, "I took out a second mortgage on my house to buy into this place for her. I used every penny I've got and promised what she has. I'm in hock up to my butt. That's how serious I am about it."

"Oh."

He waited, but she didn't add anything, so he went on, wondering whom he was trying to convince, her or himself.

"They've reserved an apartment for her. She'll be part of a community of people her age. They have a top chef and meals are provided, either in the dining room or in her own room if she doesn't feel up to going down with the others. There are trips every week, concerts, plays, transportation anywhere anytime. Medical care is instantaneous. It's a dream of a place."

"And very expensive," Abby murmured.

"Of course."

"Does she know about this?"

He hesitated. "I've talked to her about it," he said slowly. "A little."

"But she hasn't given her okay?"

"No. She's resisting." He turned to look at Abby, anguish in his eyes. "But it's time. We've been going through this for months. Look at the way she fell and there was no one to help her for so long. She just lay there. God knows what could have happened to her. She was completely vulnerable to any crook or loony who might have happened by. She needs someone near her at all times. She just can't handle it by herself any longer."

Abby sat silently, digesting everything he said. This sort of dilemma was new to her. Her parents were still youthful and vibrant. But she realized it wouldn't always be that way. Someday she would be facing these problems. How well would she handle them?

"You know," Daniel continued, "if I thought she really was physically up to the trip, I'd do what I could to send her. Hell, I'd shake down some thugs I know if I had to." He grimaced, shaking his head. "But she can't go alone. She can't go with her friend Ruthie, who's in a wheelchair and in worse shape than my grandmother is. I can just imagine the two of them lurching around the deck of a ship together. Seven days of trying to keep from landing flat on her back? I don't think so. If I could go with her it would be one thing, but I've got this…"

He'd been about to mention the hearing that would determine his fate on the force, but he stopped himself in time. "I've got some work I've got to get done," he substituted a bit lamely.

"The article for your magazine?" she asked. "Can't you put that off for a while?"

His laugh was short and humorless. "Deadlines are deadlines," he said evasively.

"You know, maybe I could help you and together we could get it done more quickly so that you could—"

"No," he said a bit more harshly than he'd meant to. He tried to soften it with a quick smile. "Thanks, Abby, but this is something I have to do on my own."

"But…"

"Forget it," he said.

His tone told the tale. He was firm on this, adamant. And there was no use trying to sway him.

She blinked, then tried a tentative smile. She'd read the signs and knew it was better to let the issue drop—for now.

"Oh, yeah?" she said half teasingly.

His mouth twisted. "Yeah."

She lifted her chin. "How you gonna make me?"

"I don't know. I guess a quick spanking is out of the question."

Her eyes widened. "Good guess."

He touched her face. "Oh, that's right. Kissing is more your speed, isn't it?"

Her smile was genuine now. "You noticed."

"How could I help it?" His green eyes looked smoky and his hand cupped her cheek. "You were all over me after the seminar last week."

"What?" She pretended to slap his shoulder. "You wish! You're a dreamer, Daniel O'Callahan!"

"Maybe." He drew his hand away with seeming reluctance and started up the engine again, glancing back at the residence and turning away from it, then looking at Abby in the darkness. "What do you want to do now?" he asked softly.

She stared back at him, her eyes huge in the

shadows, and didn't say a thing. That in itself spoke volumes.

"Why don't we go to your house?" she suggested after a few moments. "I want to see where you live."

"My house?" The whole idea shocked him. He'd never taken a woman to his house. As a cop he thought it best not to let anyone know too much about his private life. Best to remain a mystery.

"Your grandmother told me about the house," Abby said when he didn't go on. "About how she came to live there when your parents died but that you were the one who really held things together. She's told me all about how you took care of your three younger brothers. How you held off going to college yourself until you could put them through school."

"You do what you have to do," he said shortly, concentrating on his driving.

She nodded. "Hearing about that gave me a whole new perspective on what you're really like."

He glanced at her sardonically. "Don't let it go to your head. There's plenty of evidence that I'm still the same coldhearted bastard I always was."

He didn't look over again but he had the

impression she was smiling. And for some reason that warmed him.

"Where are your brothers now?" she asked.

He took a deep breath. The fact that all three of them were in the military, in harm's way, was a constant fear he held at the bottom of his heart, but he didn't much like to talk about it. "The twins are on an aircraft carrier somewhere in the Persian Gulf. And Jack is a special ops officer in the mountains of Afghanistan."

"Yikes."

He nodded, feeling a quick sense of love for those boys, then suppressing it. "Yeah, they were all wild kids, but now they're the greatest guys you'd want to meet."

Abby thought that over for a moment. "So once you finished raising them, you took over caring for your grandmother."

He shrugged. It was no big deal. "That's only fair. She put aside her life for us."

Abby sat quietly watching him drive, enjoying the way his strong hands controlled the wheel. She knew he was anything but an academic, the sort of man she'd always thought she would want in her life. He was a man of action, not a man of theories and contemplation. But thinking about him filled her heart with emotion. He had to be one of the best men she'd ever met. That surprised her. But the more she thought about it, the more she was ashamed of herself for being so surprised.

He pulled up in front of her apartment instead of his own house, but she didn't protest. If he didn't want her at his place, that was his right. She only hoped he would come inside and stay for a while, and when he showed every evidence of being prepared to do just that, she felt a bubble of happiness rising in her chest.

She made tea and they talked, first leaning against the counters in the kitchen, then sitting on the couch in her living room. Ming skulked around the corners, giving Daniel the evil eye when she wasn't pretending he didn't exist. Abby had every expectation that things were going to get friendlier if she just gave him a little time.

But after a half hour or so, he showed what he'd really stayed for, and her spirits drooped.

"Okay, Abby," he said, putting on his no-nonsense face and tone, "we've been pussy-footing around this for days, and I did ask you about it once, now it's time to come clean. You've got to level with me." He pinned her with his steely gaze. "Just exactly what products from the clinic have you been taking?"

Despite the buildup he used, the question caught her off guard.

"Me?"

"Yes."

His green eyes seemed to see right through her skin, right into her soul. She had a sudden sense of there being no escape. She shook her head, rummaging in her mind but coming up empty.

"Nothing. Not a single thing. I told you I don't take pills and the bars aren't really to my taste."

He moved closer, nailing her with that cold stare. "Abby, think. There must be something."

"No." She shook her head and her long earrings slapped her cheeks. Then she did think of something. She looked up at him, blinking rapidly, not sure if this would help. "Well, I did use the NoWait oil for losing weight. Though I don't consider that 'taking' something since you just put it behind your ear."

He stopped like a hound on point, motionless

but eager. "The NoWait stuff?" He frowned. "Really? When was that?"

"I started using it the beginning of last week. Oh, I think it was the day you came to the seminar and got that purple juice spilled on your shirt and—"

He was up and moving toward her room. "Where is it?" he demanded.

"On the dresser." Putting down her teacup, she rose and followed him, feeling an impending sense of doom and not sure why.

He hesitated in the doorway. "Where's that cat?" he asked her.

"Ming's in the kitchen," she assured him. "I just saw her there."

Striding into the room, he zeroed in on the little pot of oil, taking off the cap and sniffing the contents. Frowning, he turned to look at her.

"And you just put dabs of it behind your ears?" he asked her in disbelief.

She nodded. "I fit into this gown because of it. It really does work, you know."

He looked at her, risked a quick survey of how the gown looked on her lush and lovely body, then turned his attention back to the oil.

Why had he been so dense as to rule that sort

of thing out from the first? He was losing his touch. And perhaps his mind. "What's in it?"

She shrugged. "I don't know."

He nodded again. "Okay, let me have it tested."

"Tested?" Without thinking, she reached out and took it from him, curling her fingers around the small jar.

"Yes. I'd like to have it tested. Let's find out what's really going on." He looked at her searchingly.

"I don't know," she said, tightening her hold on it. "I—I'm not sure I should do that."

He was looking at her as though he couldn't believe her first instinct wasn't to give him anything he asked for. Didn't he understand the problems this raised for her? This was quite a dilemma. Her first allegiance was supposed to be to the clinic, wasn't it? And to the man who had given her a chance to prove her worth as a professional?

And yet, she knew Daniel was right. She finally had to admit it to herself. There *was* something going on. She'd felt a bit strange using the NoWait oil. Now that she looked back, she knew she hadn't been quite herself while she was taking it. And if there was anything strange, anything that might harm people, she should be among the first to warn others.

No, her first allegiance was to the people she served. Right? And then to the clinic. And then to Daniel?

No, come to think of it, her first allegiance had to be to herself and her own integrity. Then to—

"Abby," Daniel said firmly, breaking into her reverie. "Give me the oil."

"No," she said just as firmly, clutching it to her chest.

He looked exasperated. "What the hell? I can get it someplace else. I can buy it from the clinic. In fact…" He dug into his pocket and pulled out a ten, slapping it down on the dresser. "Here. I'll buy it from you. It's already opened, so it can't be more than this."

"No." She was worried, but she was stubborn.

"What are you talking about? You sell it to other people. Why not to me?"

"You're not signing up for a complete program."

"Oh, come on, Abby!"

"Really. I can't sell it to you because you want to use it in ways that I don't approve of. You want to use it to get Dr. Richie, don't you?"

He stared at her in disbelief, then sat down on the edge of the bed, swearing softly.

"I'm sorry." She put the oil carefully in a drawer and came to sit beside him on the bed. "I'm really sorry, Daniel. I know this is a pain in the neck to you, but we both know you can get the oil somewhere else. I just can't be the one who gave it to you. Don't you see that?"

He looked down at her, his gaze hard, but he didn't say anything.

She threw up her hands. "Okay, that does it. I'm going to make sure you get an interview with Dr. Richie. I'm sure that will clear all this up. Once you've talked to him, you'll feel very differently about it all. He'll make you understand his mission and his commitment to making better lives for people."

Daniel snorted at the concept, but didn't dispute it specifically. "That's exactly what I want— an interview with the man."

"Okay," she said, speaking with a confidence she wasn't sure she could back up. "You got it."

When he didn't say anything, she put a hand on his arm.

"Tell me what you suspect," she said softly. "Give it to me straight. I want to hear it all."

Daniel stared at Abby a moment longer, then looked away.

"Okay, Abby, here's the deal. Something is making an awful lot of people act like lovesick fools. The evidence is everywhere." He looked back at her. "Am I right?"

She nodded slowly. "I didn't believe it at first," she said. "Even after our brunch in the cafeteria, I thought you were overstating it. But what you'd told me began to sink in and I started noticing things I'd ignored before. And I have to admit, love seems to be contagious at Portland General Hospital."

"And you can see that every one of those who've caught the virus have ties to the clinic."

She hesitated. "I don't know how you can say that with such certainty."

"When in doubt, I tend to use my common sense. And it tells me the clinic is the common denominator."

She couldn't help but react defensively to that. After all, her allegiances were at stake here. But she stifled the emotional response and managed to stay calm.

"So you think it has to be something the clinic is doling out to its clients."

He nodded. "Common sense."

"And you've ruled out everything but the No-Wait oil."

He nodded again.

She drew in a deep breath and went on. "Which means you think I was infected."

His eyes darkened. "I know you were."

She stared at him, her heart beating a fast denial, but her head unable to agree. "How can you know that?"

"Abby, when we met, we struck sparks off each other. Then all of a sudden, you were all over me. It was classic."

She closed her eyes, knowing her face was turning bright red. "Ohmigod."

"You can't help it," he said gruffly. "And I know enough not to take seriously anything you do or say about me."

Her eyes flew open and she looked at him in astonishment. "What?"

"Not that it hasn't been nice having you flirt

and all. I admit I've had my moments of wanting to respond. But all along I knew that deep down it was phony, just the virus talking, and I managed to—"

"Daniel O'Callahan!"

She was furious with him, appalled, and half laughing at the same time. Using both hands, she shoved him, hard. Caught off guard, he fell onto his back on the bed and stayed there.

"Hey!"

Moving with speed, she straddled him, her slinky gown hiked up to give her legs room.

"You're a fool," she told him hotly, staring down at the man she was pretty sure she loved. "And I'm going to prove it to you."

Her hands went resolutely to the buttons of his shirt and she began to undo them.

He tried halfheartedly to push her hands away. "Abby, what the hell are you doing?"

"What does it look like?" she challenged him. "You just hush and do what you're told."

"Abby." His hands covered hers and he looked up at her, his eyes clouded. "Please, sweetheart, you don't know what you're doing."

"Daniel, I know exactly what I'm doing." She

glared down at him. "I stopped using the oil last week."

His face registered surprise. "You did?"

She nodded, her gaze burning into his. "Yes. It has no effect on me now. None whatsoever."

He looked confused. "But—"

She leaned down to kiss him, stopping his words, and then she didn't want to leave him.

"It's okay," she whispered very near his ear as she rubbed her cheek against his. "I know what I'm doing. I know what I want to do. And I know how I feel about you." She dropped a kiss at his temple. "No kidding."

His hands caressed her, and still his face showed his reluctance. "But you know that we're still not right for each other," he told her when she rose again.

She smiled at him, running her hands across his beautiful chest muscles.

"I beg to differ." Leaning down again, she pressed her lips to his hot skin and his arms came around her, holding her to him.

"But we come from different walks of life," he said, still protesting, if somewhat lamely.

"No, we don't." She cast that argument aside like so much dirty laundry.

"Yes, we do. I'm used to living among lowlifes, and you're so…so…"

"So boring?" she asked, laughing.

"No, that's not what I mean."

"Never mind what you mean. I just want to kiss you."

"Abby." He took her face between his hands and looked at her with longing barely leashed by his nagging reluctance. "I don't want you to get hurt. I really can't promise you anything."

She looked down at him earnestly, putting all the affection she felt for him in her gaze. "I'm a big girl, Daniel. If I get wounded, I'll heal."

"But—"

She shook her head, letting her hair swirl around them both. "Who cares!"

He started to say something, but suddenly he was laughing instead, pulling her down into his arms and holding her tightly.

"You're right," he said, his lips against hers. "Who cares?"

Clothes came off more easily now, first his shirt, then her dress, then his slacks and her lacy underthings. He'd been aching with the need for her for days and his body was ready much too quickly, throbbing with his desire.

He had to discipline his breathing to hold it back, had to kiss her mouth again and again to keep his from going places that would quickly rip away his mask of careful control and render him as frantic as a starved animal. Because most of all, more than his hunger, more than his deep, hot need, there was the longing to treat her the way she deserved to be treated, like a woman he could love.

He tasted her mouth, her earlobes, her nipples. She cried out at how that felt and rubbed her body against his, looking surprised at every sensation.

He knew she was pretty much an innocent. Not that she was clumsy about it. But everything seemed to be new to her, every touch, every exploration, the taste of his skin, the sight of his nude body, the overwhelming wave of desire that took her as he parted her legs and thrust his way inside her, the wild look in her eyes as she started up the spiral of the most intense sexual sensation.

And then he was lost. He'd held it back as long as he was able, and now he was all plundering male taking possession of his female and staking a claim he would kill to maintain. He took her and all her beauty was his, all her sweetness, all her love. He held her, in his arms and in his heart and made her his own.

And when it was over, they lay tangled together, catching their breath, still luxuriating in the moment. He looked at her. Her eyes were closed, but she was smiling. That made him smile, too.

Lying back, he wondered what they'd done. Even if she was free of the effect of the oil, neither one of them was free of the fact that he was here under a false assumption. He was lying to her in a worse way than the oil had ever made her lie. And that was something they couldn't wish away.

Nine

"Phoebe, you look so spry!"

Abby had come up to Phoebe's hospital room and found her just returning from a session of physical therapy. The older woman had color in her face she hadn't seen before, and an energy to her movements that was new.

Phoebe laughed in response. "Hand me down my dancin' shoes, I'm ready to launch back into life." She lowered herself a bit carefully onto the bed and the physical therapist waved from the doorway, then disappeared.

"You're doing great," Abby said with genuine admiration.

"I am, you know. I'm feeling fine, too." She punched up her pillow and lay back against it. "If it hadn't been for all this dumb worrying about blood clots I would have been out of here days ago."

"Has the doctor given you a date yet?"

Phoebe nodded. "Day after tomorrow, if all goes well."

"Wonderful." She hesitated, then went ahead and asked, "Will you be going back to your apartment?"

She knew Phoebe had her own apartment, but that she had once lived in the house with Daniel and his brothers when they were younger. And she wondered how much Daniel had told her about the place in the retirement home he'd reserved for her.

"Oh, Daniel wants me to come stay with him for a few days, and I suppose I might do that, as a transition back to my normal life," she said happily. "I'll just be so happy to get out of this place and back in the swim, I'm ready to do anything that will help that happen."

"Of course you are."

Phoebe looked around the room as though surprised to realize they were alone. "Where is Daniel? Why didn't he come with you?"

The question wasn't as odd as it might seem, because Abby and Daniel had been together most of the last few days. Somehow their opera evening had opened the floodgates. Everyone was still smiling when they came down the hall, only now they were smiling with the indulgent smirks people got when witnessing a couple obviously smitten with each other.

Tonight Daniel was coming with her to a seminar she'd been promoting heavily all week. "Love is what you make of it" was the topic. Dr. Richie planned to corral all this blooming love he saw going on around him and talk about finding that perfect someone, choosing the right life partner, recognizing real love as opposed to instant lust. Abby was looking forward to seeing Daniel's reaction to the subject. And, truth to tell, she was wondering what her own would be.

Was she in love? All the signs pointed that way as far as she could tell. She'd never felt this way before. Never. And she was so happy, it was positively scary.

"I finally set up an interview for him with Dr. Richie," she said. "He's there right now. I hope it's going well."

"Of course it is. Daniel will do what's right."

"I'm sure he will." But Abby was frowning, and she had her fingers crossed.

"Well, this will give me a chance to talk to you about my cruise," Phoebe said, her eyes sparkling. "Maybe you can help me with some of the planning."

Abby bit her lip, wondering if she should get in the middle of this one. "Daniel is worried about you trying to take that cruise," she said tentatively. "He can't go with you and he doesn't think you'll be safe."

"I know." She sighed. "He is such a dear boy, but he doesn't understand. I have to do this."

She smiled at Abby and patted her hand. "You know, my husband Howard and I used to go up to Alaska on the *Northbound Queen* once a year. We had a trip planned when he passed away suddenly."

She stopped for a moment, her gaze distant, as though recalling the horror of that day.

"I cancelled that one," she said, going on. "But

I'd always planned to go again, just so that I could say a proper goodbye to the man who loved me so dearly all those years."

She squeezed Abby's hand, conveying her emotion. "And now I'm pretty sure if I don't go, I won't have another chance." Her voice was choked, but she went on. "And I must go. It feels sort of like Howard is out there, waiting for me. Can you understand that, Abby? I really have to go."

Abby's eyes filled with tears and she nodded wordlessly. She understood, and she sympathized. Somehow she had to make sure that Phoebe got her chance to say good-bye to her Howard. But was there any way to make Daniel accept that?

Daniel stared across the desk at Dr. Richie and tried not to show his distaste for the man. There was something a little too slick about him, a little too soft, a little too evasive. He'd started out asking him questions about his childhood and schooling, but the doctor was talking in circles around every subject he brought up.

"Look," Daniel said at last, impatiently. "I'm

sure I can get all your official background stuff from Abby. What I really want from you is the straight scoop on the NoWait oil."

Whoa. That certainly brought on an undeniable reaction. If he didn't know better, he would have said the doctor was suddenly quivering with alarm.

"What are you talking about?" the man snapped, his gaze shifting to the door as though he wanted to keep an escape route handy.

Daniel's eyes narrowed. "I just want the usual product information. How did you develop it? Where did you get it? What's the formula? Where is it made?"

Dr. Richie bristled. "That is all privileged information. You can't have that."

"Oh, yeah?" Daniel leaned forward. "Then how about this. Have you applied for a patent? Gotten approval from the FDA? What kind of credentials does your oil have?"

Dr. Richie looked like a cornered animal. "You have no right to ask these questions."

"It seems to me these things should be public record." Daniel's head went back. "But I'll have to check with City Hall on that."

He realized suddenly that he was doing this questioning like a cop instead of the journalist he was supposed to be. He'd better cool it. This third-degree stuff was only likely to get the man to clam up. Maybe if he could get a little more touchy-feely… He gritted his teeth, but he tried it.

"Look, I know it must be hard for you. You carry the hopes and dreams of so many people on your shoulders. They come to you looking for a change in their lives and expect you to deliver. You're supposed to be the answer to their prayers. And then you developed this product that seems to be working for a lot of people. That must give you a lot of satisfaction."

Dr. Richie's eyes were still clouded with suspicion. "It does indeed," he said carefully. "I'm quite proud of the NoWait oil. I stand behind it, one hundred percent."

"Have you ever used it yourself?"

The man frowned. "Look, I know you're supposed to be a friend of Abby's and I'm meeting with you on that understanding. Why am I getting the impression you're hostile to me and my work?"

"I'm not hostile."

"You're coming across as hostile."

"I'm sorry. I don't mean to be." He gave a crooked grin, forced but amiable enough. "It's just my manner. I can't help it, really. Maybe it's my unhappy childhood."

Dr. Richie's eyes narrowed suspiciously. "No doubt. I'm sorry to hear that you've had trouble in your past. Perhaps that might make you more tolerant of others."

The touchy-feely method worked its magic. The doctor didn't really like him any better, but he did launch into a long explanation of his past and how he'd developed into a world-famous TV personality. The problem was, the more he talked, the less Daniel felt he knew. The man went round and round in circles, using a lot of words and saying virtually nothing of substance. Daniel's eyes were beginning to glaze over. All he was getting was useless fluff, so he was actually relieved when the doctor tired of it all.

"Look, can we begin wrapping this up?" Dr. Strong said. "I've got another appointment soon."

"Sure. But first, one more question about your background info. I checked out the places you list as your home ten to twenty years ago, before you became a media star, and there doesn't seem to be any record of a Richie Strong in any of those places."

The man was actually starting to sweat. "I—I changed my name once I knew I was going into public life. My original name was long and hard to pronounce."

"I see. Exactly what was that name?"

"I don't think you need to know that."

"If I don't know that, how can I check your previous employment and addresses?"

"You don't need to check those things. If you don't believe me, go write about someone else." He stood, calling an end to the interview. "Now, if you'll excuse me, I have some real work to do." Turning on his heel, he was out the door.

Daniel didn't spend much time mulling over his meeting with Dr. Richie. He had other things to think about that afternoon—such as a meeting with the lawyer who'd been assigned to handle his case in the department hearing. He had a date now, and the lawyer seemed to think he had a good defense, but you never knew what might happen in these things. Political pressure counted for more than truth at times.

It was almost evening as he made his way to Abby's apartment, and his cell phone rang as he pulled into the parking place.

"Yeah?" he said into the phone.

"Jimmy here. How ya doin'?"

"Great. Wonderful. The world is my oyster. How about you?"

"Not so good. I took in that NoWait oil to the lab for testing like you asked me. But there seems to be a problem."

"Problem?"

He'd gone to the clinic and easily purchased his own little jar of the stuff after Abby stubbornly refused to let him use hers. Funny girl, that Abby. She had principles and standards and a fine sense of morality. He wasn't used to seeing that in most of the people he dealt with. He had to admit it was going to take some getting used to. It also meant extra work at times. But maybe it was worth it. Time would tell, he supposed. One thing it meant—he knew he could count on her to do what was right. And that wasn't always comfortable.

At any rate, he'd taken the jar of oil he'd purchased right over to Jimmy and he'd expected to get a detailed report by now.

"What sort of problem?"

"Okay, here's the dope. The techie thinks there's something funny about the stuff but he can't quite pin it down. It needs analysis he can't do, so he's sending it over to the university. They've got a state-of-the-art lab over there and he thinks they might be able to get to the bottom of it. The only drawback is it will take a week or so to get the results."

"Oh, man."

"Yeah. I know you wanted something quicker than that. But it can't be helped."

"I guess not. Thanks, Jimmy. Let me know when you hear something."

"Will do."

Daniel put away the phone and sat for a moment, staring into space. He had a feeling this was going to be it. NoWait oil was going to be the culprit. Funny. Instead of triumph, he felt a sort of sad resignation. Maybe it was because he had that damn hearing on his mind. When you came right down to it, the hearing was going to impact his life a lot more than the verdict on NoWait oil.

Then he thought of Abby and his spirits rose. Leaving the car, he strode quickly to her door. She opened it before he'd finished knocking and she was in his arms before he had time to take another breath.

"You smell so good," he murmured, holding her close and burying his face in her hair as they awkwardly made their way into the living room, clinging together like Velcro.

"And you feel so good," she countered. She pulled back and looked into his face. "How did the meeting go?"

"The meeting?" For just a moment he thought she meant with the lawyer, but then he remembered that she didn't know about that. "Oh, with Dr. Richie?"

She nodded, searching his face for clues.

"It went okay, I guess."

She waited a moment, then went on impatiently. "So how do you feel about…things?"

He released her and slumped onto the couch, grimacing. "Feelings are not what we're going for here. We need to use the old brain. Thinking. Facts."

"Sorry." She made a face at him and sat on the

arm of the chair. "Well, then, what are you *thinking*?"

He shook his head and looked up at her almost apologetically. "I'm thinking the guy is as phony as a three-dollar bill."

"Oh, Daniel." She winced. "Did you give him a chance?"

"Yes, I gave him a chance. And he gave me nothing but lies and evasions. The guy is not a straight shooter from what I could determine."

Abby bit her lip and looked away, obviously in a certain sort of anguish over this. "I wanted to believe in him," she said softly.

"I know you did, honey." Reaching out, he pulled her onto his lap. "I'm sorry." He kissed her softly, then smiled into her sad face. "Forget about that for now."

She nodded. "I've got to start getting ready for tonight's seminar," she reminded him. "It's a special one. You're coming, aren't you?"

"Sure." He nuzzled her neck and sighed. "But you know what? I'm hungry as all get out."

"I could whip you up an omelet, but it will have to be a quickie. I've got to be at the seminar by…"

"Hmm." He touched the tip of her earlobe with his tongue, making her squirm. "That's not what I'm hungry for."

"Ah."

She laughed softly, looked at the clock and sighed as she turned in his arms. His mouth was on hers and she opened to his kiss, opening her heart at the same time. His hands slid up under her shirt, cupping her breasts and teasing her nipples, making her cry out as quick desire shot through her.

"Oh, Daniel! Not in front of Ming."

He lifted from her and stared groggily at the cat.

"Ming," he commanded, "get thee to a cattery."

The cat stared back for a moment, golden eyes inscrutable, but then her ears flattened against her head and she slunk off down the hall toward the laundry room.

Abby laughed and abandoned herself to Daniel's caresses. As he pulled away her clothing and explored her body, she closed her eyes and let herself sink into sensation. His touch was so wonderful. She'd never dreamed it could be this way.

She'd thought she wasn't made for love. Her past experiences consisted of a few furtive near-disasters and nothing very satisfying. It was always a bit embarrassing, a bit humiliating.

But this...this was so different. The way he touched her made her feel special, adored, cherished. He made it very clear that her body excited him, that as things built to a climax, he got wild and crazy with need for her. But she never got the feeling that the sex was all he cared about. It was always him and her, not him and generic "woman" set on earth to fulfill his needs. He was making love to her and she was responding in kind.

She loved him. She loved the way his mouth felt on her breast, loved the way his fingers found her most sensitive areas and stroked her to arousal, the way his hard body took control of hers and sent her to the moon.

He towered over her as she lay back on the couch, and then he was plunging into her and she took over, wrapping him in her body, taking possession of his soul for that final moment of ecstasy.

He was hers. At least for now.

* * *

The seminar was even more crowded than usual. Dr. Richie's fame was spreading and people were flocking in to see what he had to say about life—and to pick up some NoWait oil. Daniel surveyed the crowd and had a sinking feeling in the pit of his stomach. He wanted to warn them all, but he had no leg to stand on without those test results.

Looking around the room, he saw a lot of people he knew, including some who were familiar with his role as a police detective. He saw Arline looking very friendly with a handsome young intern, and Carrie Martin looking nervous in a seat by herself. The sight of Wilbur Mason wasn't surprising, but when he saw Ella sitting beside him, his jaw nearly dropped.

He couldn't resist ribbing her a little and he made his way to the seat just behind her and leaned forward.

"Ella Crown, what are you doing here?"

She looked back at him and grimaced. "If you can't beat 'em, join 'em."

"Ella, tell me it isn't so. I never thought I'd see you surrender to the cupid faction."

She glared at him and jerked her thumb toward her companion. "Wilbur talked me into it. He said the doc might be able to help me calm down a bit and not be so cranky all the time."

Daniel grinned. "He said that and you let him keep his head?"

Ella turned so that she could talk to him without being overheard. "You know, it's not all that much fun being cranky. I figure, what the heck. I'll give peace and love a try for a few days. I might even like it."

Daniel laughed and patted her shoulder before rising and heading back to the outer fringes of the room where he could keep an eye on things. Then he settled back and waited to see if there were going to be any fireworks tonight.

Carrie's hands were shaking and her heart was beating very fast. This was going to be hard. But it had to be done. Dr. Richie—her ex-husband—was winding down his lecture. It was time. If she was ever going to do it, it had to be now. She had to get this over with because she couldn't live with this burden hanging over her any longer.

Rising from her chair, she started for the front

of the room. No one tried to stop her. She saw the stairs ahead and she mounted them. Looking up, she saw surprised faces on the stage. She turned toward the audience.

"Hello, everyone. I'd like to be allowed to make a statement."

"Ms. Martin," Abby said from the rear of the stage, smiling at her with a worried look in her eyes. She was coming toward her as though she was prepared to escort her back to her seat. "I'm sorry but—"

"I have something I need to say about Dr. Richie," Carrie said urgently, her voice louder now. "Please let me say it. I just have to tell you all what I think of Dr. Richie."

The rest of the staff on the stage, obviously thinking this was going to be some sort of a testimonial to the doctor and his work, began to smile and encourage her. Abby followed their lead, but she was looking more and more worried.

"Well," Dr. Richie said graciously, smiling at her, "if you feel you must." And he relinquished the microphone to her.

Carrie looked at him. He was giving her the smile he reserved for conquests. He must be thinking she'd had a change of heart from the other day at the bus stop. She yanked her gaze away. She couldn't look at him if she was going to get through this. Gripping the podium with all her might, she tried to keep her knees from knocking. Looking up, she began.

"Ladies and gentlemen, I've known the man you call Dr. Richie for over twenty years. I knew him back in Apopka, Florida, when we both were kids. I probably know him better than anyone else in this room."

The faces were still pleasant, turned up to her expectantly. She went on.

"And I'm sorry to tell you, Dr. Richie is a fraud."

There was stunned silence for a moment as people looked at each other and waited for the punch line that was surely coming. When it didn't materialize, gasps were heard here and there among the participants. The staff onstage was paralyzed with horror and astonishment. Dr. Richie looked stunned.

"What are you talking about?" someone called from the audience.

"This is what I'm talking about," she said. "I

know a lot of you love him. I know you depend
on him. It's all very well if you think his products
and his methods work for you. That's wonderful.
And that's just what I know he wants. But I think
you have to know the truth about him. A life based
on lies will crumble and poison everything and
everyone around it. And the lies must stop."

There was a murmur in the crowd and everyone on stage was looking toward Dr. Richie, obviously waiting for a sign from him as to what
they should do. But Dr. Richie was standing as
though rooted to the ground. He was staring at
Carrie and looking white as a sheet.

"I know you believe your Dr. Richie is wonderful," Carrie was saying. "And I know he really
wants to be everything you think he is. But it's
time to tear away the curtain. Richard is a flawed
human being, just as we all are. He's not the perfect paragon you think he is."

"Sit down, woman," someone called furiously
from the audience. "Who are you to say these
things about him?"

Carrie lifted her head and went on. "My name
is Carrie Martin," she said. "But it was once Car-
olyn Strokudnowski and I was married to a man

named Richard Strokudnowski. We loved each other very much, but we had different goals, and our marriage was torn apart. I went my way and married a man named Ralph Martin. Richard went his and became a fitness guru named Richie Strong."

The gasps were louder now. Carrie kept her gaze firmly toward the crowd. She knew she wouldn't be able to go on if she saw Richard's face.

"I'm afraid my ex-husband has been presenting himself as something he isn't," she said. "He has his talents, but medical miracles will never be among them. Richard always tried hard, but he was all thumbs when it came to chemistry. He could talk you into anything, but he couldn't get formulas right. He couldn't even manage to make a decent oil and vinegar dressing when we had dinner. And he had to retake several courses in the process of getting his doctorate in Nutrition Systems. He doesn't tell you that. And he didn't graduate from Harvard as it says on his brochure. Actually, it was the University of Jasmine Island off the coast of California. A decent place, but hardly the prestigious institution he claims."

By now she had the full attention of the crowd

and the staff. She felt it and she took a deep breath, forcing herself to relax a little.

"He was never much good at facing reality," she said. "If you read his material, you would think that he was a miracle worker. He lists a string of marvelous results he claims he's had in the past. Well, let me set you straight. He can't work miracles. Those things he lists are exaggerations. He will do his best for you, I'm sure, but you must be careful of anything he tries to get you to use and you must take his advice with a grain of salt and understand that anything he recommends is just an experiment, not a cure-all. And with experimentation there are often unforeseen consequences."

"Like what?" a voice from the audience challenged.

"Beware of the NoWait oil," she said, her voice gaining power. "Haven't you noticed that people who take it are changing before your eyes?"

There was a sudden commotion and people began to cry out. Looking over her shoulder, Carrie saw Dr. Richie disappearing off the stage into the back area. And then Daniel O'Callahan was charging the stage and running out the back way, obviously in pursuit.

Carrie slumped against the podium, all energy suddenly drained. It was over. Richard was unmasked. Perhaps he was ruined. She wasn't sure. But she was sure what she'd done was the only thing she could do. The lies had to be countered with truth. That was the only way he could go on and maybe do it right the next time.

But she still hadn't told him the biggest secret of all. She hadn't told him that they had a son together, a son he never knew about. That would have to wait for another day.

Abby sat staring at her hands. She'd been doing that for hours, it seemed, but she couldn't make herself get up and do anything else.

Ming jumped in her lap and looked up into her face with a worried meow, but she didn't notice. She stared at her hands.

Her mind was filled with Daniel and Dr. Richie and Carrie Martin and the fact that her life had pretty much melted away tonight. Dr. Richie wasn't what she'd thought he was and Daniel wasn't what she'd thought *he* was. The two most important men in her life were both frauds. Where did she go from here? She wasn't altogether sure she could handle this.

When the bell rang, she knew it was going to be Daniel. What was he going to say to her? What could he say?

She felt wooden as she went to greet him and she let him in without a smile. He searched her face, then swore softly.

"Did you catch him?" she asked.

"Dr. Richie? No. He got out the back way and locked a steel door. We had to go back around and by the time we got there, he'd already driven off. The state troopers are looking for him now."

She sighed, nodding, then looked into his face. "Is it that I'm just so stupid?" she asked him quietly. "Or are all the men I deal with really good liars?"

He winced. "I guess you've already figured it out, haven't you?" he said.

"That you're not a journalist? That you're a cop who was investigating Dr. Richie all along?" She turned away from him. "Yes. I got the general idea when you took off after the doctor the way you did, but others in the audience who know you filled me in on everything I didn't know." She turned back and stared at him, her eyes clouded. "It's somewhat humiliating to be told by perfect strangers that the man I've been sleeping with is not who I thought he was."

He winced and took a deep breath. "I'm sorry," he said softly.

She shook her head. "Sorry isn't good enough."

"What can I do to make it up to you?"

She closed her eyes. "Be that other person. Turn back the clock and tell me the truth this time."

He took her by the shoulders. "Abby, I'm the same person. Honest. The only difference is—"

She opened her eyes and glared at him. "The only difference is you're a liar."

He pulled his hands back and stared at her. Pain shivered in his gaze, and then a sort of anger. Wordlessly, he turned away and went out the door.

And that was when Abby finally could cry.

An hour and a shower later, she was making plans. She had to get out of here, she had to get away. Things were so confused. Did she still have a job? Was there still going to be a Healthy Living Clinic? For all she knew, the hospital might want to jettison the whole enterprise and start over with a new staff.

Funny how suddenly success didn't seem like

the most important thing in her world any longer. There were more important things than getting prizes.

The phone rang and she stared at it, letting the answering machine pick up.

"Abby?" The voice was Phoebe's. "Abby, I need to talk to you. Please call me back as soon as possible."

Abby stood where she was, debating. Should she talk to Daniel's grandmother? Or should she cut off all ties to that family as quickly as possible? It was a big decision. It might even determine the rest of her life.

Daniel opened the door to his cold and empty house and threw his briefcase on the table, shrugged out of his suit coat and stretched, trying to get the feeling of doom out of his head. He'd spent too many hours in a hearing room for the last three days and he was sick of it.

"Gram?" he called out, wondering why everything was so dark and quiet.

He'd brought his grandmother home from the hospital a couple of days before and settled her in his guest room. It had been nice to have someone to come home to in the evenings. But now there was no answer.

Frowning, he took the stairs two at a time and looked into the bedroom his grandmother had been using. It looked too neat. And then he noticed the note pinned to the pillow. He picked it up with a bad feeling coursing through his veins.

To my darling Daniel,

I know you are dead set against me going on the cruise to Alaska, but I am just as determined that I have to go. Daniel, my dear, your grandfather is out there waiting for me. I just know it. And I have to go to say a proper goodbye to that wonderful man. He deserves it.

Now you mustn't worry. I have a companion with me. My safety is assured.

And don't worry about the money either. I had a little nest egg stored away that you didn't know about. I can handle it on my own.

I'll call you as soon as we get back. Please don't be angry. This has to be done.

Your loving grandmother

P.S. By the way, my companion is very trustworthy. In fact, I think you know how dependable she is. It's Abby, darling. Now your worries should be over.

He stared at the note for a long time, then swore, crumpled the paper and threw it down on the bed. He was feeling betrayed—by his grandmother, by Abby, by the system that had him going through these hearings that he didn't deserve. If he ended up losing his job, he would have to pull out of the retirement-home commitment he'd made in his grandmother's name. There would be no way they could afford it. And then what? He didn't know, and right now he didn't care. He needed to sleep. Maybe after he did that he would be able to think clearly again.

Ten

The air was cool enough that Phoebe and Abby needed light jackets, but sitting on their deck chairs, holding umbrella-topped virgin daiquiris and gazing out at the snow-white face of a glacier, they were as happy as any refugees from reality might be. But that didn't mean they were in complete agreement.

"I think you're being bull-headed about this," Phoebe was telling her younger friend. "Things are not as black and white as you paint them. You have to listen to other points of view before you make your judgment call."

"But, Phoebe, he lied to me." Abby took a long sip of her drink and frowned unhappily. "He had plenty of opportunities to tell me the full truth, but he didn't trust me enough to do that."

"Listen, honey, you want to know about truth? Here's the truth. That boy's had a hard life and he's done pretty well with the hand he's been dealt. But it's made him wary of life, suspicious of being hurt again. He doesn't trust much of anybody."

"He only needed to trust one person. Me."

Phoebe gave a short cough of laughter, then looked at Abby sharply. "Well," she said, "have you decided whether you love Daniel or not?"

Abby's jaw dropped and her cheeks reddened. "I— Well, I—"

"Oh, come on. We both know how you feel about him."

"Do we?"

"My dear, you've thought about nothing else since we left Portland."

"You're right," Abby admitted mournfully at last. "You know, my whole life I've always been mostly concerned about doing well, being ambitious, making the grade. And now, suddenly, all that is out the window and all I can think about is a man who doesn't care a fig about me."

"Don't be ridiculous. He's as crazy about you as you are about him."

"No." She shook her head. "I really don't believe that. He only pretended to be so that he could find out more about Dr. Richie."

Phoebe sighed. "Don't be a nitwit. I've never seen him so in love as he is with you. Imagine his turmoil as he realized he was falling in love with someone he was basically lying to. What would you have wanted him to do at that point?"

"Just tell the truth."

"But don't you see, he was in the middle of an investigation. He couldn't tell you." She threw up her hands, beseeching the heavens. "Didn't he tell you the truth about everything else?"

Abby thought for a moment. "I don't know. Maybe."

"You're asking a lot from the man, Abby. He played things the way he thought he had to. Cut him some slack. I'll make a wager he'll never lie to you again. To the point where you secretly wish he would save you from all that truth."

Abby couldn't help but smile at that notion. She looked over at her friend. The woman had come out here to Alaska on a quest, but they hadn't talked much about it.

"And how about you?" she asked Phoebe. "Has this trip done what you hoped it would do? Do you feel Howard out here?"

"Feel him! I see him, I hear him, I dream about him at night." She waved a hand toward the glacier. "Everywhere I look, in everything I do, Howard is there. And because of him, I remember all the good times. I was so lucky to have had such a good, full life with that wonderful man. I just needed to celebrate it one more time." Her voice broke and she paused to get control of it, turning toward Abby. "And I have to thank you for helping me make it possible." Reaching out, she took the younger woman's hand in hers.

"I'm happy to do it," Abby said warmly, squeezing her hand right back. "Besides, it gave me a chance to get away, which I really needed."

Yes, she'd gotten away and she'd had plenty of time to think things through as she stared at the beautiful scenery and ate the wonderful food. Still, that didn't solve her problem. She loved a man who'd let her think he was what he wasn't and who'd used her to his own ends. At one point she'd dared to dream that he might love her. How could she ever know for sure?

Plus she had a job in a clinic where the man who'd hired her was being investigated for fraud. In other words, her job might very well be gone with the wind. Too bad. She'd had high hopes for that job.

And suddenly she realized that she couldn't conjure up the emotion for the job that she had for Daniel. She cared about her relationship with Daniel a lot more than she cared about that darn job.

Wow. This was a first for her. This was totally new. So maybe, just maybe, the man was worth fighting for. That was a new thought and would require some attention.

"You're being a great big baby."

Ella Crown flashed her blue-eye-shadowed eyes at Daniel and skewered him with her intensity.

He looked at her with a frown, but it wasn't as surly as it might have been earlier in the week.

He'd been coming by the hospital every day to find out the latest on the Dr. Richie investigation, which was now official and out of his hands. Ella had her finger on the pulse and he got more up-to-date information from her than he ever did from the department downtown.

Ella had cornered him one of the first times he'd shown up and wrangled all the details of his life out of him. Funny, but she'd been his main confidante ever since. He found himself listening to her advice more often than he would have liked to admit. And now she was calling him names.

"Do you really think I'm being a baby?" he asked, feeling just a bit pathetic.

"You betcha. What you expect from that girl is only the impossible. Set the bar high enough and no one will ever be able to jump over it." She sighed her exasperation. "And you expect a lot from that grandmother of yours, too."

They were in the cafeteria and there was always the risk of being overheard, so she leaned across the table and spoke more intimately.

"I've been married enough times, I know these things. You can't dictate other people's happiness for them. They have to make it for themselves.

You can't tell other people what to do or how to react to things. You can't protect them from life. People have to be free to make their own mistakes. And you have to have a big enough heart to accept them as they are."

She sat back, looking satisfied with her own wisdom.

"Now you take me. Wilbur has been after me for weeks to go out with him. The more he pulled, the more I pushed him away. I had to come to the table on my own terms. And now..." She flashed a smug grin. "Now we're going steady."

Daniel grinned back at her. "Is *that* what you call it?"

"Certainly. We're seeing each other. We're seeing what might develop between us."

"I think that's great." He laughed. "Funny, but great."

She swatted him. "Get back to the subject at hand," she ordered him crisply. "Tell me about this retirement home you've chosen for your grandmother. What's this place like?"

He thought for a moment, then scrunched up his face, looking away from her.

"It's perfect," he said softly. "It will be like

living in a mansion. It's the best place in the Pacific Northwest." He turned his gaze back on her. "And it took all the money I could beg, borrow and steal to buy her a place there. They don't come cheap."

And since he wasn't going to lose his job, he might have a chance of paying the price. At least there had been one element of good news—his hearing had gone off well and he'd been completely exonerated. In another week, he would be back at work as though nothing had happened. Sort of. At one time he'd wondered if he would be so bitter he wouldn't be able to go back and act natural. But now he knew differently. Something inside him had calmed down, as though a tension had been released. And it wasn't only because of the results of the investigation into his activities and the good things his superiors had said about him. No, there was more to it than that.

Ella pursed her lips. "Daniel, how do you know she wants to be in this place?"

He stared at her, uncomprehending. "*Wants* to be in this place? It's what she deserves. After all she's done for me, this is the least that I can do for her."

Ella made a face, dismissing that. "But maybe it's not the right fit for her. I don't take her as the high-falutin' type. What if she's not comfortable there?"

Daniel was horrified by such thoughts. "How could she not be? Her every want and desire will be taken care of by people hired to make sure she's completely happy."

Ella shook her head despairingly. "Daniel, this is exactly what I've been trying to tell you. You can't do everything for those you love. Some things they have to do for themselves. She may hate this place. You'd better be prepared for a little disappointment."

He set his jaw. "Don't worry about that," he told her, letting a little bitterness into his tone. "That I'm used to."

She was about to say something else, but a young, handsome doctor with a full tray had approached their table and was gesturing toward the open chair.

"Mind if I sit here?" he asked. "The place is getting pretty crowded."

"No problem." Ella actually smiled at the man. "You're Dr. Riley Jacobs, aren't you? The one who's taking over the Healthy Living Clinic?"

"That's right."

Ella introduced herself and Daniel. The doctor was polite but a bit gruff and didn't seem inclined to chat. That, however, was no impediment to Ella.

"So, I guess there will be some changes made at the clinic," she said hopefully, trolling for information.

The man looked up briefly and shrugged. "I suppose so," he said. "We'll see."

Ella made a face at Daniel and went on. "Are you a TV guru, too, like Dr. Richie?"

"Good Lord, no." She finally got a reaction. "I wouldn't be caught dead on one of those carnival shows."

"But you are a nutritionist?"

"I can do nutrition," he said reluctantly. "And all that well-being stuff. If I have to."

He went back to concentrating on his food. Ella and Daniel exchanged glances and Daniel excused himself.

But he had to grin as he walked away, heading for the entrance, knowing the poor doctor was in for more of the same at the hands of good old Ella. She had a heart of gold but she did like to delve into other people's business.

Still, talking to her all week had really given him a new perspective on things. As time went by, he'd found his anger and sense of betrayal fading. Maybe he had been too hasty about some things. Maybe he ought to consider the opinion of others before he went on and tried to do things for them that they might not even want done.

Squaring his shoulders, he continued out the door, walking toward where he'd parked his car. His grandmother and Abby would be returning tomorrow. And suddenly he decided to go to the airport to meet them. Once he made that decision, his heart began to thump with anticipation, and he knew he was lost.

Despite everything, he was in love with Abby Edwards. What the hell was he going to do about it?

Abby didn't know what to expect when she came into the airport from the plane. When she caught sight of Daniel, her heart leapt into her throat. His gaze met hers and she started walking toward him. He was walking in her direction, too. She couldn't take her eyes off him. She felt as though she'd been dying of thirst and he was water for her soul. She forgot all about Phoebe, forgot there were other people milling about the terminal, forgot everything but Daniel. She began to walk faster, an urgency to reach him taking over, and he was walking faster, too. Another ten yards, another few steps, and then she was in his arms and he was holding her so tightly and swinging her around in a circle and she was laughing and so very much in love.

But he was saying something. She made herself listen.

"Abby, Abby, will you forgive me?"

She wrapped her arms around his neck. "Oh, yes. And will you forgive me?"

He looked down at her. "For what?"

"Anything. Everything." She kissed his mouth without inhibition. "I want us to start with a clean slate. So forgive me. Please forgive me for…whatever."

"Okay." He kissed her soundly. "I forgive you for whatever. On one condition."

She looked up, startled. "What?"

He stared down at her and suddenly he could hardly breathe. "I don't know if I can get this out," he muttered, feeling as scared as he'd ever felt in his life.

"What?" she demanded, pulling on his shirt and feeling suddenly scared herself. "What's your condition?"

He took a deep breath and forced it out. "That you marry me."

He stared down at her, his eyes as wide as hers. He was just as shocked as she was that he'd said it.

"Really?" she said as though she was afraid he'd made a mistake. "Did you mean that?"

He nodded slowly. "I meant it."

Then he grinned, feeling free. "I didn't know I wanted to marry you until I saw you coming in through that doorway. And then I knew." He kissed her again. "Marry me, Abby Edwards. Marry me and have my children."

She lay back in his arms, laughing. "I will marry you, Daniel O'Callahan," she said clearly. "And I'll have as many kids as you can stand."

Someone yelled, "Yeah!" and someone else said, "Kiss her again!" and that was the first they realized the clapping they'd heard was for them. They looked around, dazed, and found themselves encircled by passengers waiting for other flights. People were grinning and cheering them on. They were both bright red in the face by the time Phoebe caught up with them.

"And here you are, making a spectacle of yourselves," she pretended to scold. "I suppose you've gone and got engaged, haven't you?"

"That we have," Daniel told her, dropping a kiss on her forehead. "You missed it all."

"Well, I won't miss the wedding," she said comfortably, linking arms with them both. After nodding to the crowd and acknowledging the lingering cheers, they started toward the parking area.

"Where are we going?" Abby asked.

"Back to my place," Daniel said.

"Your house?" she looked at him coyly. "You're actually going to let me see where you live?"

"Might as well," he said, sliding an arm around her shoulders. "It's where you're going to live, too. At least in the short run."

They smiled and kissed and seemed to have forgotten all about Phoebe, until she cleared her throat.

"Listen, you two, before you go off into your own private wonderland, we need to talk about this retirement home you've got me signed up for."

Daniel looked at Abby. "So you've heard about that."

"I have. And I've got to tell you, I won't live in the place."

Daniel was too filled with happiness to let this bother him right now, but he knew it was going to nag at him in the future. "But, Gram, you need to be someplace where you're safe and taken care of."

"I know that, of course. And I've got a great place picked out. I've already got friends there and everything." She grinned at him. "It's not as swanky as the one you picked, but it's more my style. And I think I'll be very happy there."

He stared at her, not sure if he was relieved or annoyed.

"It's okay," Abby whispered in his ear soothingly. "She knows what she likes."

He turned and looked at her, pulling her back into his arms. "You're right," he said, loving her with every fiber of his being. "And so do I."

* * * * *

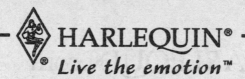

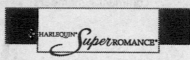

SILHOUETTE *Romance*®

Escape to a place where a kiss is still a kiss...

Feel the breathless connection...

*Fall in love as though it were
the very first time...*

Experience the power of love!

Come to where favorite authors—such as

Diana Palmer, Stella Bagwell, Marie Ferrarella

*and many more—deliver modern fairy tale
romances and genuine emotion,
time after time after time....*

*Silhouette Romance—
from today to forever.*

Silhouette®

Live the possibilities

Harlequin Historicals®
Historical Romantic Adventure!

From rugged lawmen and valiant knights to defiant heiresses and spirited frontierswomen, Harlequin Historicals will capture your imagination with their dramatic scope, passion and adventure.

Harlequin Historicals . . . they're too good to miss!

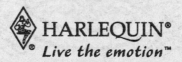

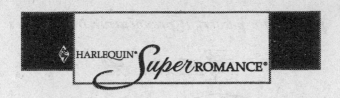

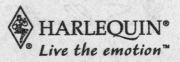